DÉJÀ VU

Juan Manuel Rodríguez Caamaño

Déjà vu

Juan Manuel Rodríguez Caamaño

First edition: January 2019

Copyright Registration Number: TXu 2- 144- 197

DEJA VU

"You never know when the worst day of your life will be, nor when it will be the best, in the face of such uncertainty the important decision is in what you will choose to think about today. "

April 23, 2018, Coatzacoalcos, Veracruz

I hate those people who argue for everything, nothing seems to them and they always have to fight even for the slightest touch of the air on their cheeks. I hate so much to argue that I imagine to be just assaulted would suffice to say, "Good morning sir, you excuse me, would you be so kind as to give me your wallet and valuables possessing?" With that kindness I would give the password of my cards so that he takes an extra of money for anything that could happen to him.

For me, the world has real problems, too serious to fight for a piece of bread, about too much noise, for a badly placed object at home, to enter first in a government agency or to be attended first at the entrance of a restaurant.

I had more than ten minutes standing in line to order food, but that intransigent woman was still arguing because the saucer that had been served was larger than she had asked. She spoke of the quality of the place, of ethics and morals, and many stupidities just for a simple banal mistake. Even menace to give knowledge of what was happening to the franchisee because, as management expert was said, a franchise must operate in a standardized manner and give the same portion and the same quality as obtained in many establishments in the country.

I was thinking at the time about the consequences of taking too long, while Alejandra waited in the car, when I had told her I would return very quickly, I would order as usual. I think, in that desperation, unintentionally and without malice, it slipped softly say almost imperceptible, "Move on".

I hope I never have the misfortune of knowing the devil in person, but at that moment that face was the most similar to what my imagination created of him, in a moment like this.

- What do you care about that?

Her eyes flashed fire, and she was absolutely right, her life was the least important thing to me, I just wanted to enjoy my favorite food; however, it took several minutes waiting to order in the bar by the foolishness of that beautiful but neurotic lady fighting. For that reason, I just nodded, with a slight and natural movement. And I felt again that flamethrower that had turned her look and also gradually her face flushed.

- Are you making fun of me?

I think that at that moment any movement I made or any word I said would be used against me, she looked at me as if I had put all that resentment in her life.

- No, lady, excuse me.

That woman was totally deranged, to channel all of her negative energy into the young man who served the fast food restaurant; she began to focus her frustration on me. Even the intensity of her anger seemed to worsen at the time in which I inadvertently intervened.

There I stayed for two minutes listening to a long and pejorative litany until I decided to just flee, it was the only way I could finish off with the problem I had acquired by not thinking before talking.

Still on the way to the exit I heard a couple of insults, wow, with what passion that woman raged, even more so with me, who had done nothing but cross in her unhappy and unstable way.

I walked hurriedly because of the cold that was beginning to be felt that January morning, for the nerve of what happened in the place and not to Alejandra waiting any longer. Snapping teeth when that combination of nerves and cold in my life was presented, it is a strange feeling, a little exasperating.

I got in the car where I met Alejandra, a bit annoyed, but more than that surprised by what had happened moments before.

   - And your churros? Where is your chai tea?

- There was a long line and I thought it better, I think I'm not very hungry, so let's continue with our plans. Besides, it's not as cold as it was in the morning when I was dying for a hot drink and my churros.

- Fuck, Martin Eduardo! You made me come here for those churros and your stupid chai tea and now you come to me with the childishness that you have missed your craving. We crossed half the city to get here, we will be late for my father's birthday and all because my boyfriend thought that today he was out of fancy and it was over.

Wow, for moments everyone would understand gays, having to deal with women's arguments on a daily basis sometimes seemed exhausting.

I think it was not my day, Napoleon used to say that "women are the only battles won by fleeing ", I had already fought a few minutes before and now I could not also run away from the woman I love.

So, I endured another temporary scolding until I decided to be honest with her, although this could be counterproductive and annoy her more, the women's classic, why you lied to me, and release another undesirable and unnecessary sermon. All I wanted was to eat something delicious and all I got was an ordeal.

- Ok, I'll tell you the truth Alita - So I used to call her when she was upset not to make things worse - I had been formed for almost ten minutes behind the person who was on duty with the cashier, who argued over something foolish and so it was , until without any malice and intention I told her that what bothered her to move on, thinking that she would finally stand aside from the line and be able to savor my favorite dish, which was even making my mouth water , just to see it, and that's why I was desperate. The crazy woman, instead of moving aside, began to argue with me and tell me a lot of nonsense. As I saw that this craziness was not going to end before the foolishness of that woman, I decided to just leave the place, leave her talking alone and here you have me, ready to drink beer with my dear father-in-law.

- What? How did that stupid girl do that to you? Good thing you told me, wait here please.

I knew that this could most likely occur; women cannot afford someone to fight her boyfriend, just them.

- No, where are you going? - My nervousness increased considerably when I saw the threat that meant that she entered that fast food restaurant.

- You wait for me here.

I could not stop her even though I tried to pull her by the arm; I knew that this was getting worse. I stayed in the car waiting for everything to be solved, hopefully and that the crazy woman had left by the other door and was no longer in the place to be found. I started to sweat like crazy while I waited for her return in the passenger seat.

It seemed that the conflict had dragged on, more than fifteen minutes had passed, and Alejandra was not leaving. I had to arm myself with courage and open the door of the car to go in her search.

Just when I was descending in anguish of the vehicle, she left through the door of that churros store.

Her face looked too pale, as if she had seen something creepy. I went to her and took her hands, they were cold.

- My love, what happened? What do you have?

- Nothing let's go - her appearance did not show that nothing happened.

- Nothing? Did she tell you something bad?, I will go to claim - I quickly pulled the handle of my door to go to face the situation and I descended the car , but she shouted to me.

– Let's go - she asked and in front of her agitation, I decided to obey.

She released her hands from mine and immediately climbed into the pilot's seat and ignited the car in a hurry.

Once we were on the way to her parents' house, she recovered her speech gradually.

- The woman apologized to me, to the cashier and also mentioned that she offered an apology to you, so there was no more reason to discuss and returned.

Ever since I was a child, I used to hear from my favorite uncle that famous phrase of "explanation not asked for manifest guilt". So something had happened inside that establishment, and I would hardly know it someday, but as I thought at the beginning of my day, it was an uncompromising discussion that nobody cared about to make my day bitter, so I better spent the whole afternoon with my future in-laws talking and drinking Mexican craft beer, the best in the world.

We had such a pleasant afternoon, ideal to start with the preparations for the wedding of which they were not yet aware.

The relationship between Alejandra and me was always very civilized. Nothing of fright, nothing of crazy, nothing of romantic fantasies, everything we did well planning and of very normal way, the wedding , that is an event that impassions a lot of people , for us it was only one more procedure, indispensable to be able to continue advancing as a couple and family.

I do not know at what point I began to hate the cheesy stuff, the last thing I remember is that I was the most romantic man in the world, also Alejandra I remember her, always romantic, I do not how it was that we changed so much. Personally, I currently hate the love details.

November 9, 2007, Coatzacoalcos, Veracruz

It was a sublime moment, of all the times I had been with her is was the first time I could feel her many orgasms, and did not know what to do or say, but I was the strongest man in the world by pleasing her.

I watched the sunset once more, with those intense colors of reddish brown, sky blue and violet, merging with the dark gray of the night that was beginning to fall. I ventured to issue a very bold number, but as far as I could see, maybe it was not so far below my prediction.

- They were six times, Bec?

I had never seen that smile on her, indeed, I had never seen a smile like that in my life – sassy, flirty, secret, satisfied - it was more than lust that gesture, retaliation what just happened over that bed of the cabin on the seashore, whose window dissipated an impressive sight, the sea to the horizon, the tanned palms, the sky totally clear, and her hair crazy on my chest.

- They were seven times Ed; didn't you feel it?

For a moment I thought she was joking, but then I realized that that was the reason why that unique smile was an unrepeatable moment that remained for the posterity of both.

The sea breeze began to approach us slowly filling us with an immense energy to get up and lie down on that hammock, exhausted and relaxed.

- Do you remember that our first time was also with the sea in the background and with the breeze brushing our skin?

- Of course, I remember, Becca! As if it were yesterday, you know that I do not want to be with anyone ever more than with you.

- Are you serious? Or is it just to keep fucking with me, Ed?

- Fucking? ha, ha, ha, I have never fucked you, when I have been with you it has been because I love you and because I have not stopped doing it with that intensity since that sunset on the beach of Boca del Rio , three years ago.
-

- How long do you think this will last? - She looked at me nostalgically with that look that weakened me and made me sincere, her tone became serious.

- Last? I never even imagined when this is over, you may think it sounds too stupid what I'm going to say, but I would like to spend the rest of my life with you - . Her eyes crystallized for a moment that's why I did not believe in the least that her next comment was true, her glance gave her away.

- That sounds very old fashion, Martin Eduardo.

- Do you really think so, Bec? So, why are you about to burst into tears? - I told her while I let out a soft laugh and she hugged me wetting my chest with some of her tears that she could not hide anymore.

So we were holding each other for a long time as we watched night came and seized everything around us with its darkness, the full moon was beginning to reflect in her smile , which created an unimaginably beautiful landscape, we listened to the sound of the wind and the music that she liked, while caressing my chest.

If at some point I could catalogue that moment it will be classified as perfect, where she and I were at the maximum, and in the context where we were , the ideal for both, would be this.

Every fraction, every second, every minute, every hour, of all the starry and shining night was simply perfect.

Maybe I was very romantic and I was too much in love with her, but I was pretty sure that this synchronization in lovemaking was due not only to a physical attraction, but to the years of synchronizing ourselves in life in so many things that we shared and enjoyed. We both loved to feel the sea breeze on our faces, so at the beginning of our relationship that started with the breeze as a witness, we set out to try to get to know the beaches all over the world, although it sounded a little exaggerated, it was a good purpose to enjoy together the places that we liked the most. We loved to eat; we constantly put on weight to delight ourselves with the delights of Mexican food, the delicious tacos of pastor, sirloin or gut. And when the weather was mild, the choice was undoubtedly meat tamales. Our favorite dessert was the Red Velvet which some occasions she prepared with her hands which gave it an incredible touch even if she was a very bad cook. That's why we used to run every morning on the soft, cold sand of the beach so as not to exceed the weight, which complemented her by playing tennis and I played soccer more sporadically and where my truncheon in the stands was always the one that motivated me to try harder and try to score in each game. We also shared our taste for movies, sometimes we could go every day to see films of all kinds of genres, being there and eating popcorn and nachos was a ritual, nor were we lost in horror even though we could not sleep for days out of fear. And what to say about the spiritual part, we both went to Mass a little bit but nevertheless we had a faith in the unbelievable God. Our dreams were very similar and always very close, even to choose a university we both plan to go to the same university in the same city. Our treatment was sometimes very abrupt, we used to joke with each other with things that we knew usually bothered us but what said between us was only part of the daily deal.

We always think that together we can survive the zombie apocalypse, she made me a fan of her favorite zombie series and we were saying that we were ready to survive that plague; she would always save my skin.

I did not need anything else in life, after sleeping in her arms that moment.

The five continents

We were always five inseparable friends who shared everything, tastes, places, hobbies, emotions, feelings, how did that great friendship begin as strong as an oak tree? I think we knew each other practically all our lives. They called us the five continents, for the amount we formed and because each one had similarities with those places.

Each had a continental feature, Rebecca, Becca as we called her, she was Europe, of a height that imposed on any man who stood in front of her, blonde and with blue eyes as bright as the Caribbean Sea, even in the character was Saxon, hard and very direct in her appreciations, she never went around the bush; Her parents were Germans and she spoke that language perfectly. From the age of fifteen she had an impressive body of a woman, which made me, and Luis have the most gross and dirty thoughts of just imagining her. Her perfectly turned legs, thanks to playing tennis since childhood, had developed the hardness and immensity of an oak. Becca turned years on April 18, her sign of Aries was sometimes very impulsive and pleasant when she left aside her rough and Saxon blood.

Alejandra was America, dark, of medium height, of an affable character like the Latins, she was celebrating her birthday every July 27, she was of the Leo sign and she made honor to it, when she got angry, she was a beast. Her parents were Oaxacan, from a town called Zanatepec, we enjoyed her birthdays very much, we ate the delicious tlayudas, and the typical dish of Oaxaca, there was not a place in the country where they tasted better. Ale was too beautiful, wherever she went, anyone turned to see her, and those brunettes from the south of our country who are struck by the golden tone of her skin with a deep look, but above all by those impressive hips.

Tere, my twin sister, was my adoration; we had been born the same day on June 27 with an hour difference since it was a natural birth, so that's why she was the older sister. We were affectionate in that we had hit the sign of Cancer. She was Oceania because her eyes were a bit torn, but her complexion was very white, and her hair was blond like an Australian Fijian mix.

Luis was born on February 7 and was Aquarius, as indicated by the description of the natives in this sign he was a strong and attractive person. Undoubtedly Africa, and although his features were not so marked Afro, his skin was quite dark, apart from having a robust body and very curly hair.

I, Martin Eduardo, was Asia, my dark complexion and the slanted eyes made to seem a combination of the main Asian races of India and China. Medium in stature, a bit sturdy because I was fascinated by drinking beer, unlike the others who always drank whiskey or vodka when there was not so much budget. I was not even very good looking, my main quality was to act as the soul of the party, said by themselves, if I was not, nothing was the same, everything was boring, so even sick I had to attend meetings and alternate some little joke with the nose dripping, in order to please my inseparable companions.

Our parents had agreed as partners of a construction company and had established a friendship of years, friendship that allowed us to always coincide on vacations in any part of the country, or the world when the company went well.

If I had to describe Coatzacoalcos, I would not use geographic or demographic terms. I would just say that its sunset is the most beautiful landscape I have seen in my life. The sunbathing the San Martin hill whose reflection on the dark blue of the sea creates an indescribable effect when merging with the infinity of tones in the sky, sometimes they are reddish, sometimes lilac, sometimes blue so light that it seems the same paradise. And not only is the visual effect, the soft and fresh breeze that the sun produces when hiding, revitalizes the body and the soul. That is a sunset on the southeastern coast of our country. The oil boom of the 80s allowed it to have even the largest petrochemical company in the country and one of the largest in Latin America, called the city of the avenues.

Despite having several brothers, we were the five who also agreed to have been born the same year, 1988. And we were always in the same academic grade from kindergarten, primary school, middle school and high school, in the same school. For many, the friendship derived from the relationship of our parents will seem somewhat boring and forced, for us not, we were a brotherhood, and we could not leave if we did not go together, wherever we went. We agree 4 of us besides being born in the same year, to be Dragon in the Chinese horoscope, which is the only mythical creature within it, whose element is the earth and whose main characteristic according to the old followers of these beliefs is the power, apart to be very social and tolerant. Luis although he was born in the same year was Rabbit, because the Chinese year in that year ended on February 17, so in theory his characteristics were more of longevity. We also coincided four of us in that our birthday ended in the number 7, June 27, July 27, February 7, only Becca met different, in 18.

That's why family vacations were always decided by us, because most of the five of us were the spoiled children in their family and we influenced the parents about some destination, so it was almost a fact that it went where we suggested.

Only once we failed to convince everyone to choose a place, even though it was just Alejandra's birthday, it won the proposal of Nacho's younger sister, Milka, who turned fifteen and had to be granted her caprice.

And yet, that was the best summer vacation trip of all, the finances were not quite right in the company so the partners decided to choose the main national tourist destination, Boca del Rio, Veracruz and thus also fulfill the dream of Milka who, apparently, had a boyfriend from that place and had talked wonders, well, I think the Veracruz of Agustín Lara was as much poetry for her as the descriptions that jarocho made of his city.

July 28, 2004. Boca del Río, Veracruz

Nothing softer than to feel the sea breeze on a summer afternoon, try the delight of that fresh wind that caresses you after receiving the most intense rays of the sun. Go from the hectic and hot of the day to the temperate of the sunset.

That city in the conurbation of the most emblematic city of the state of Veracruz, an extension of that "Little corn where the waves of the sea make their nest" as defined by the Veracruz troubadour Agustin Lara, located in the Gulf of Mexico. It was an ideal place to fall in love or to go with the person I was in love with.

"Veracruz, your nights are deluge of stars, palm tree and woman. Some day to your distant beaches. I'll have to go back. "

We were all in our 16th birthday, the most beautiful age to dream, we were always five, so we decided to self-name ourselves as five continents.

I wish we had always been five and I'm sure we would never have stopped being so happy.

Many things changed after that vacation, the first is that I lost my heart, I gave it to her.

That day we got up five, a quarter for six in the morning to run on the sand of the beach, watch the sunrise while we felt the softness of the sand of the Gulf of Mexico, nestled in the Atlantic Ocean, it was a unique experience. Even more so when Becca was by my side, all those colors that formed in the sky when the sun was rising, forced me to involuntarily take her hand with the nervousness of a boy of that age who has never extended his love to a woman and less of the one who has been her friend from almost babies. My right hand was sweating excessively not only because of the exercise we were doing, but because of the nervousness of what she might think, although she took me even stronger in approval, when arriving at the breakwaters that lead to the lighthouse, all that remained was to decipher an enigma, if she had taken me by the hand because we had a great friendship or because she felt, even a little bit, what I had felt for many years.

The boys realized that movement, but they pretended not, because they knew my character too shy with the women and did not want to spoil this opportunity for Becca to know that I adored her. Even so, they whispered slightly, but Becca, fortunately, did not notice.

Becca is the first image of a woman that is engraved in my head, I think, over my mother, I still remember her with that dress in kindergarten and her pigtails that made her look extremely tender, her angelic smile that captivated me from that moment and she still had the same unbeatable smile to this day.

On one occasion, in the second year of primary school, she approached me when some kids were bothering me and she simply, with her imposing voice, pushed them away, annoyed because they took advantage of me. I loved her from that moment and even more that I lived with her every day, for years, few people can boast of knowing each other perfectly like her and me. That's why it was so strange to have never said anything to her.

Arriving at the lighthouse with the sun at midpoint, the rays on her eyes, I approached my lips and slowly tried to touch hers so that she would realize and at that moment and decide to step aside or respond to my lips.

We kissed, that was my first kiss, it was not her first one, she was so beautiful and so lovely that she had had a couple of boyfriends in high school, which I hated to witness.

I did not stop shaking and she; however, she did everything that I could not, enjoy that beautiful kiss, in that spectacular summer sunrise on the beach.

The others, seeing the scene, went to bathe in the sea and invited us, if the kiss in the lighthouse was beautiful, it was even more so when we got the taste of salty saliva from the sea water and feeling her skin closer to me, her waist touching mine and her chest mine.

By noon, she challenged me to go with her to the parachute driven by a boat to show her that I loved her, even though

I was beginning to realize, because of the way she treated me, that she always knew that I loved her. It could not be otherwise, my way of looking at her and my concern always for her betrayed me.

I do not know why I did that madness, if I'm afraid of heights, being there in the air with her, although separated, it was an incredible experience, I really felt that we floated together at a certain moment. I imagined that they could unleash those parachutes and we would fly to the highest part of the sky and there we would merge in a kiss so tender and romantic that clouds would form with the shape of our lips.

The afternoon fell and the sunset in Boca del rio is the most beautiful landscape that exists, we began to work, Nacho and I, in making a bonfire for when the night came to heat some marshmallows there. Meanwhile, the girls prepared something light to dine with what we brought from the fridge, apart from wine and beer.

The night fell and in the light of the fire, while those three joked and talked, she stared at me.

- Why until now?

- Until now what?

- Until now you kissed me.

-I love you as a friend, almost since we were born as well as all the group, but for you that affection goes beyond that of friends, always was, since I have use of reason. I thought you would always see me as a brother so I was afraid to spoil that relationship, but believe me for me you will always be the woman who steals my thoughts, regardless if this lasts a month or a year or all of life.

-I love you too since we were kids, I cannot believe you did not notice. - Her words relaxed me and made me feel the happiest man on Earth.

-Not ever, I do not know, always your deal was like we were brothers.

-It was like that because I always wanted to be near you.

I fell in love even more with her when listening to her, and she kissed me, not tenderly, but with the passion that a woman kisses a man and we let ourselves be carried away by our caresses and the smoothness of the sand. I did not want to try anything else for fear of getting upset, she asked me why I was so tense to touch her, and she just told me that I should always take risks because we do not know what might happen the next day, we do not know if we will be alive.

We made love for the first time both.

August 17, 2008. Monterrey, Nuevo León

- Why did you decide to study psychology?

- Since I read in the baccalaureate about Pavlov's experiments I was very attracted to this theory of conditioning in psychology.

- Pavlov? What are they?

-During his research on the physiology of digestion in dogs, Pavlov noticed that, instead of simply salivating, that it was an innate response of dogs, when perceiving food or when presenting a ration of powdered meat; the dogs began to salivate when the person who normally fed them was present. Also did the same when the bell rang, with which called to feed them. With this he could realize that he could condition the behavior. He called that salivations "psychic secretions" and deduced that, if a particular stimulus was present when the dog was given his food ration, then this stimulus would be associated with the food and would cause salivation by itself.

- Sounds very interesting stuff.

-Yes, then came another scientist surnamed Skinner, who developed what was called "operant conditioning", as in classical conditioning coined by Pavlov was working on the stimuli applied in the experiments, Skinner worked on the answer; established that a person is more likely to repeat behaviors that lead to positive consequences and less likely to repeat those that lead to negative problems. For example, what our parents do if we get good grades, we try to reward and thus more excellent grades, however if the result is not desired to apply some punishment it is not repeated. This is what psychologists do to try to modify behaviors. Since I read about these issues in a magazine that has my father in his office, as I waited, he leaves work, I was fascinated by psychology and all the scope it can have on human behavior.

- I also want to learn a lot about these subjects.

- You did not know about all this?

- Not at all, I had no clues of those studies that seem very important to our career.

Gave me a good laugh that assertions Carlos, such naive to enter study at the university without the slightest idea of what is at least the graduate profile.

- ¿ So, why did you decide to study psychology?

- My mother has a mental health problem called paranoia, which she has been treated with excellent results; however, it is both her fear that she will attack us, that she decided to distance herself, claiming that she could not risk our lives if at some point her illness worsened. Since I started studying high school, I stopped seeing her every day, which hurts a lot and that's why I looked for a career with which I could support something to her suffering. My first choice was psychiatry but not passed the exam of medicine at the Autonomous University of Nuevo Leon, so I had to choose a related career and because I was told several acquaintances that psychology was the option most close.

- I'm sorry about your mom - I felt sorry for having judged his career choice without first knowing the reasons that led him to take such a decision.

- Do not worry, she is much better, and I hope that at any time she returns home. And why did you choose the Tec de Monterrey to study? It is very far from your city.

- I do not know, I think for many reasons, my dad studied here and with honors, which was a challenge to prove that I was as capable as he was. On the other hand, I believe that being away from my family would make me more responsible; On the other hand, if I studied in my city, the party would be the order of the day. Monterrey, capital of the state of Nuevo Leon, is the land where my father was born, his whole family is from here and I have always thought that it is the most developed state in the country because of the culture of its people. They have copied the best of American culture of responsibility at work with the simplicity and spontaneity of Mexicans. This remote land in the north of the country, Mediterranean, with scarce natural resources became the motor of Mexico for the effort of its people. And the last reason is that my girlfriend which I have been for four years of happy relationship also will come to study here because his father 's family lives here, but I do not know why the last minute changed or of opinion and went to study in Mexico City. It broke my heart that she did that, but I did not want to interfere in her decisions, so we decided to do our best to frequent us often, either traveling to Mexico or her here to Monterrey.

- You did not ask for what reason changed her mind?

- No, I did not want to invade her privacy, nor influence her decision. Love must be totally free, that's what my parents have told me all my life. If someone is going to be with you, she would do it in spite of everything, without needing to ask.

- Tell me obtrusive, but I think, in my very personal point of view, that you should ask her reasons, obviously not interfere with anything, but you should question her about her change of choice.

- I've thought much the same, but for right now we're here studying so as not lamenting is good, someday, at some point we're together and relaxed I'll ask and send you a text message at that time, you will be the first to know what the reason was.

- Ha, ha, ha, are you telling me gossip?

- No, I'll just clear your doubt. The next class I think is up in the afternoon.

- Yes, Perception, why don't we go to that bar, the only one that is close to the campus, which they call Classroom 8.

- Ha, Ha Classroom 8, why do they call it that?

- It must be because the classrooms only reach 7 and it must be the place where most students attend.

- But, how will we arrive with breath alcohol for the afternoon classes?

-Still missing four hours, we go, we just took a bite to eat and came back here to the central cafeteria.

- Ok, let's go.

December 24, 2008. Coatzacoalcos, Veracruz

Arrives colorful, indescribable and majestic, one of the most important celebrations for all Mexicans, acculturation of Catholic religious beliefs and our indigenous culture. That is why, after November 2, when we pay homage to the dead, everything around us begins to draw another color, the frequent black becomes the bright white of winter snow, of births, of houses adorned with lights of all cheerful colors that exist. It is the most emotional time of year is when even the hardest hearts melt down.

That would be the crudest Christmas of my life, my sister Tere spend the holidays at her boyfriend, was understandable, both were still devastated, how to spend a Christmas alone missing our parents in every corner of that big and cold house, which became so by their absence only five months ago, in that terrible plane crash. From that day I decided never to travel by plane. I do not know if for fear of seeing my parents sitting there covering me with a blanket because of the cold like when I was a child and traveling to all parts of the world.

I could not condemn Tere to live the solitude that I would spend in the house on Nayarit Street. There where we put the tree all together for years, where we distributed the gifts on December 25 very early, where we ate tortas and tacos leg and turkey overheated as dictated by tradition, which states that it is better tasting than freshly cooked.

So, I even pushed her English boyfriend to take her away from here on these dates. This ordeal of memories and sadness had to be faced all alone. Even so, being away, she would also have a very strong emotional blow to the awakening was 25 and did not hear the voice of my father when he spoke either in the bedroom when children or a phone call , demanding us to get up already for breakfast very early. Only he could get up at 6 am on December 25, after watchfulness, and thank God it was up to eight in the morning that began with the ritual of awakening the family.

For me it would be a severe blow just the fact of being the first Christmas that they would not be with me. So I did not make plans, I just pretended to attend a celebration so that the people who loved me would not worry, and go to sleep early, buy some fast food dinner, a bottle of wine, watch the fights of the UFC and to sleep in that bed where I often slept in their midst when I was a child.

And that day arrived and had not yet bought Becca a gift, but would see her until after this year dying, should think of something, so I went to a mall and look for a bracelet to combine with almost everything she had and that she always could brought her with me and she remembered me. I asked for it wrapped for a gift and I placed it on the tree to evoke happy Christmas.

- Hello baby, how are you?

- Becca, is that you?

- Who else is going to call you? Of course, it's me, what are you doing?

- Sorry, baby, I fell asleep.

- Asleep? But it is six in the evening of the eve of Christmas, who sleeps at this hour?

- I guess me. I lay down for a while because latter I will go to the neighbors to dinner. - I tried to hide that I had not anything planned to not spoil her Christmas.

- With the neighbors? But if you do not know anyone in the colony, you are too pathetic! Wake up and hurry it is about to rain out here and I'm going to get wet.

- Outside? Where are you?

-Outside of your house babe, open me.

My heartbeat with emotion like never before, in that difficult moment she was there. She ran down and brought a bunch of grocery bags that led to the kitchen and immediately opened it.

-What are you doing Becca?

-What do I do? Preparing the snack that we'll have for dinner.

-Dinner? Baby, you should be having Christmas with your parents; you have no idea what it is to spend Christmas without them, not that I wish to anyone.

-Who says we're going to spend Christmas away; they know everything that has happened, and you know my parents adore you and were great friends of your parents nearly 30 years ago and decided to come and spend the Christmas eve with you.

- With me? Where?

- I do not know, at the hotel or here you decide, but since we have little time to prepare everything.

- Well, let's do it here.

She stayed looking at the tree and found her gift. She tried to take it, but I stopped her, until it was twelve o'clock.

I remember we prepared the snack; we fixed the table and an hour later her parents arrived home.

We all cried when Christmas arrived and place the baby Jesus at birth, my parents were like brothers of hers, every hug of them was as if my father and my mother wished me a happy Christmas, was it more like a complete Christmas. We drank wine and talked many anecdotes that time flew until three in the morning when they parted to their hotel.

She surprised me once again; she walked her parents to their car and came back to me.

- What are you doing Becca?

- What do I do? Well, I'm saying goodbye to my parents so we can sleep now.

- Are you going to stay with me?

- And what did you expect? Of course, so take a bottle of wine to the bedroom and something to snack on.

We hugged all night and cried much, went from being the sadder Christmas of my life to something we could not say the merrier, but the most memorable for so many mixed feelings, and above all, by having her always at all times, in the most complicated situations of my life.

November 2, 2010, Coatzacoalcos.

Since Valentine arrived at the group as the sixth in discord, I sensed that things would not go well.

He saw my Becca in an unusual way, that time on the beach I saw clearly with my sunglasses on, that he undressed her completely with his eyes, well, I even noticed some slight reaction in his body.

I remember that day I had a very important soccer match and I was so upset because Valentin from the first moment did not stop flirting with my Becca that I decided to invite a secretary from the office to cheer me in that game. Becca as always, arrived on time and wished me good luck while I wanted Maritza to arrive so that I would cause Becca jealousy and feel like I had felt earlier that day. The party started and my guest did not arrive, I saw her appear for the half of the first time and immediately I watched Becca bother but greeted her politely but with that cold and lethal smile that she dedicated to people that she did not like, she did not even greet Maritza's mother accompanying her daughter. I saw them exchange words for a few minutes and Maritza left the place pale. I knew that Becca had done her thing as always, so direct, impulsive and hard. When the game ended, she ran more loving than ever to hug me although she hated to do it when I was sweaty, but she hugged me and kissed me, I knew it was her way of compensating me. Immediately I asked for Maritza and she simply replied, "Your friend had to leave for another commitment", at the time she also apologized because her parents had called her, and she had to go home. She retired without giving me a kiss and I knew that my play had gone wrong and that she had become very angry because I gave priority to another woman asking for her and not paying attention to Becca at the end of the game. I paid dearly for the mistake; it took two weeks for her to agree to go out with me.

The next day when I asked Maritza why she had left, she answered that my girlfriend had told her that she would not tolerate any slut that would come looking for me and that she would either retire or be unemployed. I felt so sorry that I tried to invite her to lunch but she refused and asked me to please only speak to her for work reasons. And so, I lost a friend from work.

Becca always said that I was a flirt and that for that reason one day I would lose her, her jealousy sometimes became irrational and always kept away all my female friends, except those she knew and also considered her friends. The reality was that I liked to get along with everyone, and yes sometimes I was too kind to women, but it was in my nature, my father was the same. That did not mean that I was going to change her for another one, she was my life, we were a team together, invincible.

When we met Valentin there was no longer the same privacy, we had to talk about what was uninhibited, just because there was a stranger in the group. That, although he tried to fit in, only Alejandra liked his company, his comments were sometimes so unpleasant and distasteful that Luis and I chose not to frequent that bar where we always met the five, now six. Until it arrived a moment that by the occupations of each one and as it was the only place where we agreed, the brotherhood went away.

We saw each other every month, then every two months, then just to celebrate someone's birthday, give him his gift and that's it.

We stopped being an inseparable group , all for let someone in in our team, we could not deny Alejandra to tread who wanted , but should have foreseen this and put rules to meet only the five of us at the bar always , though each who already had a partner. That missed us and we lost contact, from more we coexisted with Valentin, was the kind of guy who had the heavy blood, saying things without respect for anyone, overbearing, in more than one occasion almost hit our waiter not to serve what he asked, he was one of those guys who would never want to meet in life and, however, arrived to our life and stole our Ale.

We should never have allowed it.

December 17, 2010, Coatzacoalcos.

 The sun warmed the leaves of bougainvillea's there all along each corridor of the beautiful gardens in Becca's house. So many times, I dreamed that she and I lived here; the gardens that for years cultivated her mother were the cutest that I had seen in the world. I wanted to one day get up and be the lord of this house and have tea here on the terrace, surrounded by millions of flowers and a beautiful blue sky like Becca's eyes. And how not to have that desire, perhaps something presumptuous, if for several years ago, I did not even know how many because I do not remember the first Posada of the season away from this house, her parents prepared a simple celebration for a light dinner while the mariachis played around our table. It was practically my home and her parents as if they were mine too.

The last time we had some German-style sausages courtesy of the lady of the house and they fascinated me. We drank German wine; we could not choose another in that house. more or less between eleven and eleven thirty of the night that his parents went to sleep we went out to have fun at the usual bar with the five continents, there we sometimes woke up depending on the day of the week in which it fell, if it was undoubtedly Saturday we would be there until they played some bolero and they would rush us from the place.

And although having breakfast and lunch with my family and toast until dawn to then go to the boardwalk to watch the sun rise were beautiful moments, the part that I most expected was always to have dinner at Becca's house.

And even more than months ago on my most recent birthday when I felt that she no longer paid attention to me as before and her parents told her to attend to me as always. They had a great affection for me.

I think it was my 17th or 18th birthday when Becca cooked dinner for me, that was the worst-tasting dinner of my life, the meat was about to be completely darkened due to excessive overheating but nonetheless I ate all that done by her hands made me feel that I could enjoy a banquet and a pleasure that nobody else could achieve. Because she loved me, and I loved her. I did not emit even the slightest complaint so as not to make her feel bad. On the contrary, I served several times meat and that unusual and quite simple combination of salad to show that it was a delight despite her lack of cooking skills. However, her brother Jaime who also accompanied us that day broke the charm and began to make fun of her inexperienced seasoning, so the dinners she made were debut and farewell that night; she never wanted to do it again from how badly she felt thinking that I had spoiled my birthday for unimportant nonsense.

At these ends of the year dates I always became more nostalgic and with feelings on the surface, and she was always close to me.

- Take, your gift, baby. - Becca handed me a small gift bag. Open it to see if you like it.

- Baby, you know that everything that comes from you always pleases me. – I told while I pulled out of the bag a beautiful black thin tie.

- I hope so, although I do not know if you like the color.

- A black tie, baby?

- Yes, it fascinated me since I saw it in the distance, at that mall store in Shanghai.

- I love it, but I almost do not use the color black baby, I do not like, you know me better than anyone. I do not have any clothing of that color, I do not like white either.

- I know, but I imagined you with that tie and a black suit and wow, I felt that I got wet to see you dressed like that, you looked super sexy. Besides it is original Chinese silk and it cost me a fortune, but that did not matter because I want to see you wear it at a special event that you have and after that take it off wildly and the rest of the suit as well.

- Ha, ha, I like the idea and when am I supposed to use it? We do not have any formal event soon.

- There will be an occasion, do not worry, there will be a perfect opportunity to use it.

December 24, 2012, Chihuahua.

That winter was one of the coldest in Chihuahua. The state with the largest territorial extension of the country, border with the United States of America, which borders the states of New Mexico and Southwest Texas. It was part of what I had memorized in Geography class since elementary school. Cradle of the only man who has invaded the USA and lived to tell it, the famous Doroteo Arango, better known by the name he used not to be persecuted for justice, who stole a man he found dead on the road named "Francisco Villa", the great Pancho Villa. A historical state too. I wanted to meet it as a child for those reasons, now my reasons were different, if there was a landscape that I considered romantic, it was a winter sheltered in a cabin in the mountains, and Chihuahua seemed to meet all these requirements to be away from the world, only she and me, looking at the mountainous and icy horizon to enjoy each other and reflect on our relationship. We decided to spend together some time after leaving our last vacation in college, almost about to graduate me in Monterrey and she in Mexico City, I believe, it was the last Christmas we spent happy from that moment on the cusp that we met, where we understood each other perfectly, we synchronized like nobody else to do anything: play, talk, make love, hug, walk on the street, understand each other, it started to come down.

We toured several places in this beautiful state, but what more I liked were the hours spent on the train to Creel watching snowy landscapes but covered with blankets and cuddled almost all the time in the cold and drinking red wine with her.

I breathe deeply. So deep that the fresh air of a too-chilly morning merged gently with the delicious steam of coffee aroma and with its light perfume adhering to the scent of her relaxed skin. Yes, it is the most pleasant aroma perceived by my senses; I baptized it like her, Becca. At minus three degrees below zero dawned on Christmas Eve I got out of bed again feeling the touch of her hair and her neck to remove my right arm from under, to serve me a cup of coffee that had put to warm minutes before. I opened the window completely without worrying about the cold that I could counteract by adding more wood to the fireplace, that landscape could not be lost, that immense snow mountain of just seeing it shook the skin, the toasted flavor of the coffee poured into a clay cup and her silhouette asleep among the rumpled sheets of that large wooden bed.

Through my mind I spent my whole life with her as I watched her, hundreds of moments with her throughout our lives as friends and as a couple, from the worst in which she scolded me for any nonsense and remembered what sometimes irritated her way of thinking. to argue for anything, in fact to convince her to spend time together was an intense fight, she did not want to come here with me in the first place, she was going to travel with her classmates from the university to New York to also spend the new year there in what is supposed is one of the most traditional places to start the year, Time Square. The incredible moments like when we were stuck in that elevator of a shopping center were also going through my mind when we were still just friends and she hugged me again and again afraid and I was happy that she squeezed me with her arms. I could make a balance by number of good and bad moments, by the intensity of them, by the duration, by the frequency, but the balance was always the same, her smile won.

She had decided to come with me, so I had to make a difference. I went to the kitchen, everything was ready, I served it on a wooden tray and put it on the table on her side.

I gave her a kiss in the mouth with her morning breath that although it might seem unusual I liked, she woke up and the first thing she saw was that Dutch tulip, her favorite flower, in a vase on a tray accompanied by a coffee, obviously from Veracruz , her favorite dish prepared by me, French toast. I had never cooked but I took great pains to use ingredients that I had already tasted and that were almost ready to be used like that Canadian maple honey that she loved. So, decrease the chances of not liking it. She stared at the flower and pulled me by the neck to kiss me and throw me on the bed.

- Baby, your breakfast that I prepared from very early is going to cool down.

- What do you prefer to cool, breakfast or me?

Definitely no matter how much I thought about how carefully I prepared that breakfast since five in the morning, the way she kissed me left me no other choice. And is that the intensity with which she kissed me was not for lust, but I felt was not wanting to leave me and that's why she did not separate her lips from me. I only reached with my right hand to light the horn next to the bed and I heard that melody that she did not like at first but that eventually became almost a hymn.

"A small part of you is enough for me,
To be the happiest man,
Just having you here with me
I can feel love just like that."

My appreciation was certain she wanted to be with me hugging me just to feel what I already knew by heart that I could be with her always, that's why she hugged me for a few minutes while being inside her and she laid on my motionless chest without making any gesture just squeezing strong with her arms.

-What will we do next winter?

-First enjoy this, right? - I started to make fun of her and she put her classic face intimidating me.

- Well, then I'll go with my friends since you do not think to book me from this moment.

-You are always reserved for me. And of course, I already have a plan; I'm waiting that tickets for the concert of a Welsh group called Stereophonics go on sale and that you and I love. - I said it while with my index finger I slowly went to her ribs to tickle her.

-Seriously? Can you imagine listening to "Dakota" live? Thousands of people chanting the end at the same time.

"I don't know where we are going now"

"Take a look at my now"

-Yes, I imagine the two embraced and shouting the final chorus of our favorite song.

- Ours? It's my favorite song strained, yours is "Million reasons" by Lady Gaga. - at that time, I put my finger on her lips as a sign of silence containing laughter.

-Shhh, baby, please do not tell anyone that I love it, what will they think of me, that's a song for teenage girls.

-It's a nice song and you like it because I dedicated it to you even though I've seen you have not paid attention to the lyrics or you would not like it at all.- and at that moment her voice is a serious imitating a manly voice.- for an alpha male silverback leader of the Hess Sala tribe.

She kept laughing and he was making fun of me.

-Now it turns out that we are the Hess Sala tribe, it should not be upside down I am the man and the father's last name always goes first

- Gender equity baby, apart let's be realistic you are the lady in this relationship, and I am the strong man who protects the herd.

She had a grace to say things that's why I adored her, all the nonsense she could come up with in a heartbeat, that creativity I had never seen in anyone I knew.

We spent the whole day reading in the cabin embraced, she read a new book by a novice author "Always You" by Juan Manuel Rodriguez Caamaño, while I read the teacher Juan Rulfo, I never tired of reading "The pain in flame ", we drank coffee all day, for moments we laughed or we were distressed reading and we asked each other the reason and we told each other funny or sad parts of the book so we decided to end up exchanging. We both finished reading at the same time when the sun was already setting, we exchanged the books to keep them in our suitcase and read them on another occasion because it was time to prepare for Christmas.

Cooking together was an incredible experience, even the atrocious scolding that I took to burn the donuts without wanting to, and that she was not an expert but in relationship women are always right. We follow to the letter the instructions to heat that codfish to the exact point for dinner. We would drink with the drink that we always celebrate our anniversaries and special dates, mezcal, accompanied by orange slices and spicy worm salt. A delight, I better dedicated myself to cutting the oranges so as not to spoil anything else and that she would bear the total responsibility of the cod. When I finished cutting, I prepared the rustic wooden table with tablecloths, candles, cutlery, and sat down at the table.

>-Look how comfortable the man, already sat down to wait for his housekeeper to serve him.

>-Baby you said that I do not serve for the kitchen, so to not do more damage to the dinner I did the operative part and sat down.

>-You're right, much better, but capable that the codfish would taste like turkey.

We both laughed and I gave her a kiss. We sit at the table and pray. She prayed to thank God for that happiness and for having me, which reminded me of the important thing that I already knew was for her. The dinner was delicious even the fritters burned with honey had a nice flavor. We symbolically put the baby god in the manger for lack of one when it was midnight and Christmas began.

Right in Christmas eve it started to snow and what was missing in our fake wedding log was just that, a kiss under the snow. We had already kissed so many times in the rain, the wind and the intense sun, but snow was something new in our list of moments to live.

We cheered as ever, maybe we were not as excited as the first-time making love, but, nevertheless, that night we did several times as we had not done in a long time. And each time was better because we already knew each other perfectly and we knew how to shake the other.

Christmas morning we wake up to open our gifts and prepare coffee and breakfast to stay in bed all day, I loved to spend all day holding each other, lying around doing nothing, only watching the landscape, talking about any nonsense, but feeling her close to me as my support, always.

- What did you ask for Santa?

- A star-shaped pendant, I'm sure it comes on this horrible wrapped little box that I found next to the tree heh, heh.

- You joker, I took great pains to wrap it up, but I'm not an expert, baby.

- Do not worry, baby, and what did you ask for? - I knew in advance that my response could generate a strong reaction in her; my curiosity was whether it would be positive or negative.

- Nothing material, just asked to be all Christmas next to you. – A tear ran down her cheek combined with a tender smile.

- You can consider it a fact. - And she hugged me very hard until her tears disappeared and we went out to see the beautiful and snowy landscape that was outside the cabin.

June 5, 2013

I thought about using the tie that Becca had given me to attend my graduation as a psychologist. However, the terrible news that she would only attend a couple of hours at my graduation made me keep that tie in the last drawer, I was about to throw it in the trash.

The excuse, something stupid, was that she should be very early on Sunday at an event of her university, the farewell to the newly graduated students. For me there was no justification, I had missed the football final of my varsity team for attending her gradation.

I even hung up the phone the last time we talked, so it's likely that the night was uncomfortable for both of us.

Luis, Alejandra and Tere could not miss this important celebration, at 9 pm we were all sitting at the table, and with everything and she would only be a few hours at the party and then take a plane back to Mexico City, Becca had not arrived.

For a moment I thought that her courage had been such that she had decided to return sooner. This made my anger at that moment because she still did not arrive to be transformed into fear, into a huge fear that the most important person for me was not present at such an important moment.

In the delivery of titles barely and I could greet her quickly because her flight arrived delayed and left the airport directly to the venue to just give me a big hug to take a picture with me that made me promise not to publish because she was dressed casually after the trip, and from there she said goodbye to go to get makeup at her hotel.

It was 9:30 p.m. and she still was not arriving and there were very few empty spaces in the Convention Center, where all the attendees looked very elegant. Fortunately, the festivities had not started yet, the group that would entertain the party was just arriving and while played reproduced music.

Everyone asked me about Becca, my uncles from Monterrey, my cousins, even the stupid Valentin.

-Hey, Ed, what about Becca? Is she coming?

I did not even answer him, I just pretended I was not listening, and I turned around and went to say hello to family members of career colleagues who had been arriving.

I looked at the clock prostrate in the high part of the room 9:37 at that moment I felt her hand touch mine.

-Sorry to be late, baby.

I felt that I could not avoid complaining, my courage was such that I could not let this opportunity to let her know that she should not fail in the most important moments of my life as she had never done so far.

I was shocked to see her, I fell silent, I swallowed all my words, the moment I saw her face, that hairstyle made her look more beautiful than ever, that dress of a light color that I could not define what it was, with an opening that let me see her imposing legs, an elegant but impressive neckline, each accessory perfectly combined with her perfect features, it was like making the moon shine more, all that effort to look spectacular was reduced to a simple moment, her blue turquoise look that made me flooded in that ocean.

- Ed, tell me something, please. I did what I could to be ready as fast as possible, even more I changed my plane ticket for one that came out a little later and get straight to the event of my career, do you apologize me?

I continued stunned like a machine that was congested with so many conflicting emotions. I remembered our previous dances, the graduation from elementary school when she was my dance partner, the dance of the high school where we were still great friends, the graduation dance of the high school that we were already in a relationship, and once again we were here she and I, face to face, she being a spectacular, incredible woman, and I trying to be the man who was at the height of what a perfect woman requires.

-Ed, answer me.

-I love you

She hugged me tenderly; she had not noticed how impressed I was to see her again after a couple of months and in these circumstances.

-I love you too silly; I'm going to greet my parents.

At that moment I heard the song that we liked so much, and I took her from the waist to dance.

- What are you doing Ed?

- It's been a while since we did not hear that song together, so let's dance for a moment.

She smiled but she took my hand and started to dance that song called "Tenderness" that had accompanied us in so many moments. I felt that my heart was beating too much as if our relationship started at that moment, as if we had not spent a whole life together, it still made me nervous to have her body near, that emotion was fantastically indescribable.

I made the most of the three hours I spent with her, it was not long so I was not going to waste a single second arguing with her, I did not dedicate a second to anyone else at the party, I knew that once she left I could enjoy the other guests, but meanwhile it was only Becca's.

Time flew by and she said goodbye, I begged her to accompany her to the airport, I did not want to get rid of her.

-Don't, Ed, please do not do it, I would die of pity that you would leave your relatives for going to leave me, they are here for you. Please, my love, I promise to see you soon, we can already be together all the time, I decided to accept my father's proposal to work with him in Coatzacoalcos, just as you will.

That news was better than receiving my Psychologist degree that night; I could enjoy that look every day. After telling me that, I no longer insisted on accompanying her and I returned to enjoy with a huge smile on my face every second of my graduation until dawn.

-You have not removed that stupid smile all night, Eduardo.

-You want to have this smile of an idiot lover-

-Ha ha, that smile is stunned not in love.

-Think what you like, what do you know about love, dear Luis, if you have had a thousand women and with none of you have had the chemistry that I have with Becca.

- You're frightening me, Ed, please don't tell that you want to get married.

-With Becca I would marry tomorrow.

-Ed, you are 23 years old and just finished the career, stop thinking about those crazy things, you have a whole life ahead of you.

-Life that I do not want to live far from her, you know better than anyone, you've been all your life close to us. Thank you for always being here, thank you for coming to my graduation.

-You know I would not miss this for anything in the world I'm not, Becca hahaha

-You're a son of a bitch, but that's how I love you.

January 17, 2014, Coatzacolalcos, Veracruz.

Contrary to what I thought, these last six months in which supposedly things would be like before, when Becca and I lived in this city and enjoyed doing everything together, it was the opposite.

Why? I do not know. I only know that sadly we frequented less than even when we were separated by a thousand miles. For months I wanted to think that it was the routine of having to work, unlike when our only responsibility was to enjoy together, and part shared long hours of class in the same room for more than ten years.

I came to think that our estrangement at this time was circumstantial because of the excess of work we had with the economic problems that the country was experiencing and therefore the enterprise of our parents. Sometimes we did not even meet at the office, our job was to be outside reviewing each of the projects, and we barely had enough time to cover them all.

In that same way every time I was harassed by the question, would not our circumstantial infatuation have also been? We were born the same year, we studied together for years, our vacations were together, our free time in the city were among our families which forced me to spend every minute of my life near her.

I shuddered to think that while I breathed the hot aroma of the vapor that came out of my american coffee contrasting with the cool of winter that was seen through the window, the cloudy afternoon and the dark sea water stirred like every one of my thoughts.

Then I began to reassure myself, that my thinking as a psychologist was always that in life everything is circumstantial, simply had it not been for the circumstances I would not have known her, I would not have been her dance partner in the kindergarten graduation, elementary school, middle school, high school and university.

Circumstantial yes, but even if we were stuck all day or were the only beings on earth if there was not that chemistry that we had to get along in everything, it would not have been possible to be together.

I was grateful to the circumstances and to God for having put her on my way, for that sunny summer afternoon when her father and mine met in a job interview and when they were both accepted in that multinational they went to celebrate at a nearby bar and in that moment was born that friendship that later would be translated into entrepreneurship as a company and a few decades later in knowing the love of my life.

I decided to break the leisure in which I found myself that was the source of those stressful thoughts and I better called her to take advantage of Sunday and to attend to see a movie at the cinema with her, she could not deny it was something that we loved to do.

From the outset, she alleged that she had many pending works, but I insisted once again and a little annoyed by her refusal to see us until she accepted.

When we saw the billboard there were several attractive premieres that we both wanted to see, we chose without hesitation to see that with that program of putting back old movies was Vanilla Sky. We had seen it so many times together, in her parents' house, in her apartment in Mexico City, in my house, and now we had the opportunity to see it on the big screen like we could not do at the time when it was new.

We both cried every time we saw it but this time was the exception, only I felt a lot of nostalgia with the film and even seeing that it had not caused any havoc on her I stopped myself from doing it more loudly.

We walked in the park around her house talking as always when we went out to see a movie.

-First time you do not cry when we see this movie, Becca.

-I do not know, if you see it with logic, how will you fall in love with someone who you only met one night?

-Ok, Bec, but it's a beautiful story in the context, it has always fascinated us for the same thing, because probably you only know the love of your life for a short time and do not need years to realize that someone will be the person you are looking for. Well, that's what I think.

-After years of seeing it and with maturity, I realize that it is a superficial love, Ed, think about it, you only know that person one night that is magical, fascinating for both but because a whole life remembering that moment sounds like a martyr.

-Yes, you're right, it cannot be compared with our relationship of years of knowing each other and being together, that's true love. - I took her by the hand and tried to kiss her and just touched her lips briefly and she moved away.

- I have to go, tomorrow I have to get up very early to go to check the part that we have of the project of the Transistmic Corridor.

That was undoubtedly the most important project in which our construction company was participating and perhaps also the most important for the country and I was extremely proud of her because she was the leader of our group in the project. From Hernan Cortes had glimpsed the possibility of bringing the two oceans in the narrowest part of North America that was precisely the Isthmus of Tehuantepec, that strip that goes from the port of Coatzacoalcos, Veracruz to the port of Salina Cruz, Oaxaca. After more than four centuries that project was being carried out and for that reason, I understood her obstinacy in doing it in the best way, I knew that by ending this I could already think about making a family with her.

-Of course, Becca, do we eat tomorrow?

-I do not know, I'm saturated with this and you know it.

Her response altered me a bit; I should not have pressed her.

-Is that it, or do you no longer want to eat with me?

-I do not know either; perhaps we should give us a time to finish our projects and to miss us.

Miss us? If I already missed her a lot, she was not the same as before and each time I missed her more. At that moment, her parents parked outside the house to greet us, they had been arriving from a dinner and they were very happy to see me.

-Hey Ed, do not think about it much, we already want to see our grandchildren.

-Don't worry, sir, if it was for me, I'll marry tomorrow with your daughter. - Becca made a false smile when I mentioned that, I knew her too much.

-It seems perfect! Have an excellent night.

They said goodbye to me and Becca took advantage of that moment to give me a quick kiss on the mouth and say goodbye, I gently pulled her arm to ask her to go the next Sunday at the cinema too, had checked the billboard and put another classic that I liked very much "Eternal sunshine of an spotless mind".

-I know you like that movie a lot, but I do not like it that much, it does not make me anything romantic that someone cowardly flee from a relationship by erasing her from his memory.

I always thought that she also enjoyed watching it with me but apparently not anymore.

-Ok, we will see another one. I guess what you said was a joke, right?

-No, Ed, think about it. I really need some time to focus on what I'm doing, and you put a lot of pressure on me. So, I ask you to respect my decision to take some time out of the relationship.

She said goodbye to me fleeing behind her parents and I stayed outside of her house while blowing that strong wind from the north that was not so cold but at that moment I froze and more touching my face wet from a couple of tears shed by the effect of her painful words.

I could not sleep all night, I felt that every day that passed I lost her a little more, every time I saw her, she was colder, more insipid, I despaired of not being able to do anything to return to be the perfect couple we always were . I would not wish anyone that despair of feeling that you slowly lose who you most want, for moments I calmed down thinking that it was only because of the workload and that in the future everything would return to normal but then I saw this as an idealist and pulled me the hair thinking about losing her.

Maybe her father was right; I should definitely take that step to be with her forever.

June 4, 2014. Coatzacoalcos, Veracruz

- What's your name?

She deciphered clearly, with the tone of her question, the undesirable intentions of that stranger, so she answered only out of courtesy.

- Becca

- What a nice name!

With that compliment she confirmed that he was trying to woo her, which was forbidden for her principles. So, she answered in a molest tone and ironic.

- My name is Rebecca, but my boyfriend tells me Becca.

- Wow, he must be extremely lucky to have such a pretty girlfriend and romantically presume how he calls her.

- Of course, I'm very lucky to have him, even more, I hated my first name, until he started calling me Becca and from then on everyone else. I passed from hating that name to love it from hearing it first from his lips. You do not even imagine how lucky he is, because not only I am his girlfriend, but I also adore everything done from him, every moment, every day. - She thought, foolishly that with that clarification the bold guy would stop meddling in her life and look for some other woman.

- You're not going to ask me what my name is? Even for the most common courtesy.

- I'm not interested in knowing it even if it of courtesy. Otherwise, I would have done it.

She had no idea what kind of person she was joking with.

- Leobardo Garcia at your feet, though you are not interested to know, I'm sure at some point you may be interested and if so then, we can have dinner together and talk about any nonsense, I can be your best friend.

- I do not see any apparent reason, neither now nor in the future, unless you are also a defender of the cause of the local abandoned children.

She made the mistake of revealing one of her greatest weaknesses, mentioning the name of that altruistic foundation that she had formed to help homeless children in the city, he found a loophole to enter her world and therefore little by little in her mind.

- I'm not, but if you teach me how I can help, I could be a great defender of that cause.

- Well, unless your interest is genuine, you can be a promoter of a very important cause for the future of our city.

- I also believe that helping children of this city, that's my interest to know how I can be useful to the cause mentioned by you, tell me what is needed in that place and tomorrow I analyze what might be my contribution.

She finally smiled, seeing that the attraction for her could be channeled to support what she wanted most, those homeless children.

- It really notices your ignorance of what is happening in the city, these children lack about so many things that their needs are an endless list.

- If you write down each and every one of those needs here on this napkin - he spread that piece of paper subtly and with a worried frown, pretending great interest and tapping to gently touch her hand.

She took it and began to write down a list that completely filled one side of the napkin.

* Specialist doctors,

* Medicines for different conditions,

* Psychologists specializing in child therapy,

* Nutritionists,

* Food pantries with each of the children's favorite ingredients.

- With that is enough, or can I continue on the back?

- As you wish, although I would like that you let me that napkin and give the address of the foundation and let me review what I can get of all this and later you ask me for the rest. Agreed?

- Ok, I think it's perfect, - she sketched another smile, more beautiful than the previous one, she knew the value of making that gesture at that moment to get the support for her children. - Well, nice to meet you Leobardo, is that your name?

- That's right, Leobardo, Leobardo García, do not forget, that name could become very important in your life, obviously I mean the support that I can represent in your foundation. - The smile of Becca was of grace and no longer of mockery, as previously and she walked away to her work.

The next day, when she arrived at the foundation in the afternoon, which was the time dedicated to The house of the port children, she found a great hubbub of all the volunteers, who congratulated her for having obtained great support, at such a degree that they could never have imagined. That day there were not enough supplies to organize, schedule consultations, pack medicines and food. It was a dream day for the foundation and also for her.

Becca knew that there was only one way to pay all those exaggerated and expensive attentions for each of the children of the foundation, which ran joyfully through the garden of that old house and who loved them as if they were her children, so she had to remunerate that splendid favor and call Leobardo to thank him for his attention and concern. Her voice was no longer cutting, on the contrary, trying to look as nice and kind to him.

- Hello, I was just calling to tell you that the other side of the napkin is missing, with the other requests from the foundation.

- Seriously, a heartfelt apology miss president, I forgot to review that end, but I have no major problem in reviewing that list today as at eight o'clock in the night you leave the foundation, in the cafe located on the corner of the boardwalk, I have understood that the cappuccino of that place is your favorite, so that you will clear your mind to draft a long list and do not miss any requirement, tomorrow or any while I live I'm alive.

Although Becca knew that those attentions were due to his interest in her, she was willing to continue with that romp while she managed to see those eleven little angels smile in her care. But in spite of everything, that voice was no longer as unpleasant as in the beginning.

- How do you know I can at that time? I probably already have plans with my boyfriend; my time out of work does not mean I do not have other commitments to attend.

- God! I do not think that you cannot sacrifice a date with your boyfriend, who you see daily, to achieve even more support for this noble struggle we do.

- We perform? Ha ha ha, since when you are already a part of it if you have one day that you know about the project, but ok, you're right, wait for me out there the foundation at eight o'clock, I'll prepare my list of demands for the hour.

- Look, I know you think that I act like this just to try and conquer you, which is partly true, but I want to tell you that since I had the chance to be there present in the foundation you've convinced me to support altruistically . And look, I do not know if something can happen between us, but it is the least important, you have no idea how good I feel performing such actions. And do not worry about carrying infinity of requests; I will also carry a very special request. - Becca did not know the tricks that the new acquaintance could wield to seduce her.

- I do not know if I can do it, maybe my religion forbids me to. - She laughed, an ironic laugh, apparently there was more confidence between them.

- Calm down, it's not that you sleep with me, it's just a smile of yours, I hope you can satisfy that requirement, but I'll be reluctant to your requests. - And he answered with another laugh.

- How daring! How do you tell me those things so strong, but hey, let me think about it and if you behave well, I'll give you a little smile?

Undoubtedly that contempt felt by Leobardo at first; with his attentions, coupled with the mysterious personality of this new benefactor, they were attractive to her.

July 7, 2014. Coatzacoalcos, Veracruz

I woke up lying on that huge bed of the most luxurious hotel in the city with an impressive headache. I was completely naked and tried to remember what had happened one night before.

My body ached and almost drank with a sip the jug of water that was on the furniture aside of the bed.

For moments I passed blurry images of what had happened the previous night, I knew my body and the worst of all is that I felt totally dirty because I could feel that I had fooled Eduardo for the first time, I always thought that I would only be with him in my life and for a night of drinking everything had changed.

I could not blame someone else, even if I had it, I had fallen into this trap myself, since I decided to go out with Leobardo. I knew it from the moment he came to court me the day we met; his intentions were to seduce me. He did everything that was in his hands, approached to me subtly under the pretext of supporting my project and, managed to endow the foundation of everything needed to make those children happy. For that reason, I felt so many mixed emotions, I had drunk numerous times until I lost myself and I had never lost consciousness to do something I did not want, therefore , I could almost swear that he had drugged me to access any pleasure.

How could I see Eduardo again after this? Although our relationship was falling into monotony, leading it into a deep slump, even which though sounded like an excuse, was the cause for which I had agreed to go out with Leobardo.

I took my clothes and got into the shower where he had left several gifts; some flowers with a card: "I hope this is the first of infinity nights we spend together," I was disgusted to read that words, and think there could be more nights like this, I felt sick. I stayed almost an hour feeling the water run over my body, as if expecting it clean the dirt from my soul and my thoughts to remember some moments of those unwanted kisses.

How could you do this Becca? I questioned myself over and over again, and the answer was the same, I had made a serious mistake, and the mistakes are paid dearly. Did not want to leave this luxurious room for fear of seeing some familiar face when leaving, who was known or not, I felt that my dirty look betrays me of what I had done, to the slighter gesture.

So, I took my coat and ran out of the place to the elevators, luckily, I did not see anyone there, when opening the lift, I rushed towards the exit and what I least wanted to befall, passed.

- Miss, are you ok?

- Yes, great, thank you very much.

The concierge has approached to me and at that moment I felt all the looks of the hotel guests remained prostrate on me, and guilt again take over my body and kept me walking in a hurry to get to the parking lot, got into my car where I felt the most big relief when I closed the door and started the engine.

I left the parking lot and took the avenue that crossed it, at that moment a call entered my cell phone. It was Valentine, it was the first time he called me, I thought maybe something had happened to Alejandra and I answered immediately.

- Hi!

- Hi, Becca, are you behaving badly?

I became extremely nervous with his assertion and was about to hang up the call. My subconscious was betraying me, since he had no way of knowing what had happened.

- Why do you say it? I'm coming out of an event.

- At 6:30 am? Wow, there is no doubt that in that hotel they have 24-hour attention. Do not worry, your secret is safe with me, but let's have breakfast and talk.

Valentine's voice sounded very friendly and not to arouse suspicion I agreed to go to breakfast, we chose a place near the boardwalk to enjoy the view of the sea.

- What were you doing there, outside the hotel? Were you spying on me?

- No, I have not slept at all , I had a lot of work yesterday, in fact, my office is opposite the hotel and so I saw when you came with your new friend, the famous gangster Leobardo "The Lion", I think that is how he's called.

His confession left me cold, he had realized everything that had happened that night, however, he hugged me.

- Do not worry, we're friends, but take care, you know that guy is dangerous, and I would not like you to get hurt.

- Yeah, don't worry, I will not see him more, and Alejandra?

- I do not know, we broke up, we decided to give ourselves some time, we are very good friends, but we did not work much as a couple.

We chatted very pleasantly, and we said goodbye after a big hug.

In the afternoon I remembered that I had forgotten in the hotel the bracelet that Eduardo had given me on our third anniversary, for which I decided to return with the face of shame that that moment generated me.

There was Valentin, again out of his office and he realized when I arrived, so I decided to say hello so as not to arouse suspicion.

He came over and I explained what had happened, I was no longer ashamed after confessing my folly, he felt like a great friend, besides it was a very handsome man and took great care of his image, dressed impeccably and the care of his physique was also noticeable. He hugged me, and leaning on my car, very tenderly offered to accompany me, much better, he made all the management to ask and go find the my bracelet to the safe box, and I just waited sitting in the lobby while drinking a coffee.

Fortunately, my bracelet appeared and immediately I put it on my wrist, we take a coffee there in the lobby, and at the end he walked me to my car like a gentleman and opened the door for me.

I got in, and when he closed the door I felt him kissing my lips, I tried to move and avoid it, but his lips were so soft and he generated much confidence as a great friend , so I got carried away for a couple of seconds in which the kiss became a little more intense , I pulled myself away from him.

- Valentin, what are you doing?

- Sorry, Becca, excuse me, you're an amazing woman and you fascinated me.

- But you had a relationship with my best friend and I'm with Eduardo.

- I know, I'm sorry, seriously, it will not happen again.

I spent the whole night meditating on that kiss, trying to make it just stay in that, a coincidental kiss of two people who probably felt alone at that moment, and more after what I had lived a night before when I needed a true friend and Valentin seemed so, with the defect that it was also obvious that he wished to be with me.

I fell asleep deeply, with so many mixed feelings of what had happened these past two days, sometimes going through my mind, feeling that I was the worst human being and I felt very dirty, then I realized they were things that tend to happen and they serve to learn and not to make those mistakes again, I even had a nightmare where I lost Eduardo forever, and although I no longer loved him as years ago, it hurt, we had spent our whole lives together , I knew no one better than him and him me, it hurt me so much that dream, even woke up crying when the alarm sounded.

I got up and dialed Eduardo, I wanted to see him, only he would comfort me as he has always, at the most difficult times of my life, did not answer me and I insisted, surely he was still sleeping or was upset by my decision to have a break so that everyone clarifies their feelings.

I don't know at what moment I made that decision, it's like when you are drowning and instead of looking out there, you do everything possible to sink more.

Yes, I called Valentin.

- Hello beautiful, how are you? Seriously, I apology for last night, I promise it will not happen again, do not know how sorry I am.

- It's not true, you do not feel sorry, so at least that apology requires that you add an invitation to go to breakfast together today at the hotel lobby in front of your office.

- Sure - the voice of Valentin was normal, complete surprise, he did not know what changed my attitude. - I'm already here in the office, you tell me when you arrive, and I cross the street to see you.

- Ok, I think it's perfect, we'll see how sorry you feel, I'll see you in a while, kisses.

In that moment and after what had happened to me, I did not want to be alone. My heart was shattered because I was so confident with Leobardo, I never thought he could abuse me that way. I accept that yes, I was a little flirt with him, but that was no reason to take advantage of my unconscious state and get me into his bed. I felt so dirty, I needed Eduardo by my side to comfort me, but he did not answer my calls. Valentin was the only person who knew what had happened to me and I felt completely confident that he would support me in this difficult moment of my life.

July 8, 2014, Coatzacoalcos, Veracruz

I had already known few in the last months about her, we only greet each other briefly in the office when we met, at first I let her spend time thinking that she would realize that no one was going to love her and treat her like me and she would come back looking my affection that always had at all times, happy, sad, terrified, nostalgic, euphoric. I felt for a moment that foolish security that men feel when we believe that women, being in love, always have to be with us and do what we say. I think I was wrong to leave her alone these months; I should have been like on that trip to Chihuahua when things were not going so well, and I made a difference trying to be everything she wanted. This time it scared me, I was terrified to think about doing it again, procuring her and falling in love every day and that even then she would not want that. So I bet on the easy, which did not involve any commitment, which did not involve any effort, but nevertheless it involved an emotional wear every day waiting for a message from her, a call to give me good morning and wish me success in my draft. I did not either because I did not have any sign of her and I had to do it, she had a thousand more reasons for me to send her a message of support, her work in these months with that colossal project was greater than mine, I did not tell Becca how proud I was of her, that I not only adored her for the time we had spent together, but also to see what she had become, a successful independent professional who could have immense responsibilities. But I was afraid to be there,

I was afraid of rejection. I felt safe after so many years of being in her life and in her family practically, I felt that I had that place won at the table in her house with a cake every day of my birthday. No one could take away from me the place I had obtained for years, that I thought for several months in which I imagined again and again in my confused mind that I did not have to do anything to deserve her now, as if we had signed a contract where she should be mine for life without doing anything in return, without having to water that flower every day. How stupid I was. After months of crazy ideas I began to believe that it was impossible for her to leave me alone for not being in love with me, it was clear that there was someone else in her life, so I followed her that afternoon when she exited her job.

I saw them enter that elegant hotel and my heart had never felt so much pain, much more pain than anger because , although I wanted to kill them with my own hands, the wound was so big that I was devastated, immobile, helpless, in that storm that was hitting. The rain did not stop, and it made me feel cold or maybe it was just the effect that that discovery had caused on me.

I stayed there nearly freezing, all the time thinking a lot of explanations, from the most incredible, to avoid pain and seek an acceptable solution, they had been there for some logical reason, perhaps preparing some surprise to

Alejandra for Christmas, perhaps thinking of a surprise to me.

And yes, it was a great surprise for me when they returned to that place again, in search of something they had forgotten, in the distance I thought I saw that he was carrying in his hands that gift I gave her.

My God NO!

And then that farewell was not the usual, they kissed each other on the lips, she sat in the pilot's seat and he stood outside her car, which made me shudder with disgust. It was the first time in my life that I felt that inexplicable energy that made me tense with desire to destroy everything around, feeling each vein of body burning, but with all that energy I was paralyzed a scant fifty meters from them and I could not run and hang them with my hands that was what my mind drew every fraction of a second that his lips were close to hers.

Why Becca? I dedicated my whole life to you, and you pay me like this just for being separated for a few months, it's unfair, and whoever decided that this happened was unfair to me. So I put the fingers of my hands on both temples and I began to cry in a way that choked me, I lacked the air in each attempt to inhale the pain, I felt that my lungs did not work, I tried to scream but my voice was also annihilated by that energy so strong that it ran through my entire body.

They moved away from the place and I remained trying to recover my strength to go in search of them, but I took a long time standing there crying. When I could breathe without so many complications, I would never reach them, I walked to my car and there I sat with the seat reclined while I thought about what to do. It was something that in my life had ever happened to me to live, so I did not know what to do, call her to claim her, insult her, ask for an explanation or an opportunity. I thought about going to her parents' house to tell them or waiting for him to come to his house to face him.

I did not sleep through the night because of the pain of constantly seeing those images in my mind, but at least I already knew what the cause of her was abandoning me. I felt that my eye bags weighed a world, I do not know if it was the effect of crying every time that I remembered and denied it, it irritated me, it dared me, I lost the notion of reality, and that powerful energy in my body made me unable to sleep, it was a terrible anxiety that made me think thousands of crazy things and prevented me from even feeling a little sleepy or tired. With a terrible headache I do not know if it was because of so much crying or because of the courage or the sum of both drilling my head.

We had broken up so many times, but after seeing this it seemed like a real, imminent ending.

I thought of so many things to do to try to find out why, to find out when, to try to make them suffer, the way to make them regret all their miserable lives for having betrayed me; however, when I calmed down I decided to call him to claim him. His excuses did not wait, I could not even speak of the pain, combined with the courage, I threatened him, I cursed him, I made him see that I would do anything to destroy him. Contrary to what I thought and his usual arrogance, he was conciliatory, trying to calm me down. With everything I told him, anyone else would have immediately hung up the call, but he endured the gale. I felt disarmed before that and ended up reassuring myself and demanding to meet him to find out what had happened, in great detail, and he agreed.

July 17, 2014

-I'm sorry, Eduardo! I swear I tried to get away from her, but she looked for me to see us.

What a miserable guy can revile the impeccable image of a woman, he listened like a coward talking badly about her to try to justify himself, and even if I had to hate her on the outside, she was still the woman I admired the most in the world and I was hurt by the words of that idiot.

- How do you ask me to forgive you? If you killed me in life, you've shattered all happy moments with her. How could you be so vile, being Alejandra's boyfriend, who is her best friend and is like a sister to us? We were a damn family until you arrived. I do not know someone more cynical and disrespectful than you. You are a cunt.

-Yes, you're right, hate me all you want, but for something you asked me to come here to talk, tell me, what do you want from me.

-I do not know, it only killed me the curiosity to know why you had done it, to know what you did with her and where. Know how many times you saw each other and if she told you that she loved you.

-Is that all? I do not think she loves me; I think it was just a moment of weakness that she had before the pressure of feeling that she had deceived you. With me she found too much confidence, I do not know why, or well, at least I have a crazy theory.

-How will she feel pressure to have cheated on me and cheat with you, it is illogical that the future happens before the past.

-I did not talk about cheating on you.

- So?

My hands froze as I took that cup of coffee to which I added a little rum to take courage and face the truth. He was about to cry, first the blow of being in front of this little guy who was not worth a damn, and he had held her in his arms and had made her his own, as to now deal with another horrible mystery.

-Are you implying that...?

- Yes, she cheated on you with that guy of shady business that sponsored all the campaigns of the foundation formed by her.

-That is not true.

-If you do not believe me you can ask Alejandra, she knew it too, but since Becca is her best friend, she would never reveal that secret.

-And you still talk about Alejandra as if nothing, after having cheating on her.

-Alejandra and I was one more relationship of friends, we never really feel great love for each other, I confess, and she can also tell you why we still end civilized.

- Civilized? Changing her for her best friend, what a civilized guy!

-Look, you can keep trying to insult me, I do not know if you believe me or not, but I'm being totally honest with you and that responds to a reason that surely you will doubt, but I have a great appreciation and affection.

Eduardo could not believe the words of that guy who had entered the lives of his friends to arrive at that brotherhood they had. How someone who had snatched the woman he loved could have cared for him.

-And then, why did you do it? Give me a damn reason. - I rapped the table vigorously with my clenched fists of courage. -One that is credible. Not the nonsense you've told me so far.

Eduardo believed that all the words he had spoken to Valentin had made a dent because he was on the verge of tears. Deep down he was glad to see him, even a little, defeated after all the damage he had caused.

-Ok, I will, do you want to know the real reason? - He said as he nervously rubbed his nearly empty coffee cup. -Let's see then how little man you are to accept the truth and not run away from here cowardly. - He got up very nervous from his chair, put the cup on the table and went to Eduardo, approached him almost to his ear resembling was going to tell a secret. At least that's what Eduardo thought. When he was at the height of his ear, he bit it lightly and Eduardo blushed, Valentin kissed him on the lips and Eduardo by surprise or curiosity remained that way, motionless, feeling how his lips were touched by him. Until he reacted and pushed Valentin away.

- What's wrong with you, idiot?

-I told you that you could not stand the truth, if I stayed there in that group where it seemed a complete stranger was for you. I never wanted to be with Alejandra or Becca, I always wanted to be with you.

Eduardo did not let him finish his explanation and immediately left the place leaving him with the word in his mouth.

-Don't run away, do not be a coward, you asked for the truth, now face it...

July 24, 2014

My hands trembled as when the cold froze them on the mountain, but this time they sweated without stopping, for my mind had not happened at any time to live such an unpleasant experience like this, in my mind I never imagined another relationship or another woman who was not her. Facing this situation that filled me with dishonor, grief, anger, sadness, nostalgia and pain was something unpredictable what would happen next, so I thought very quietly in every word that would come from my lips and contain that hatred I felt for her and that each tick of the clock increased just thinking that someone else had touched her skin, that skin that drove me crazy and was always mine.

I let a few days pass to digest it, I was sure that in the moment my voice would have broken of sadness or anger, I would not think what I would say which would make things worse, I knew myself too much, I should think coldly every reaction of mine and hers.

I brought that book that we exchanged in Chihuahua, it was a written proof and with more than legal, moral validity, that she had sworn eternal love. Written and signed with her own handwriting.

I imagined her face when I took it for surprise of something, she did not even imagine that I was aware of.

For a moment I held back all my anger at seeing her come out pretty with that angelic smile and with that light skirt that let me see her legs that fascinated me. Her reception contrary to the last times we had seen was much more kind, my mind besieged her behavior, making me think that everything had been a lie of Valentin or a moment of weakness of her, maybe it was better to bury everything and stay with her as if nothing had happened. My hatred was immense, my rancor towards her, but my love for Becca was infinite and that could overcome any obstacle.

She invited me to sit in her living room, yes there where I always dreamed to be the lord of it, today I just wanted to go out well, to have hope, to hear from her lips that it was not true and I would believe her immediately or if she asked for forgiveness for making mistakes and I would also do it without thinking, being in front of her I could swallow my pride of the size of an ocean.

-Tell me, what is that important thing you have to say to me? You know that whatever happens to you I will be there to support you.

Those words weakened me, turned my immense pain into a miraculous ointment for the heart.

-I do not know how to tell you, Becca

-Eduardo, you scare me, did you kill someone?

And she let out a laugh that made me even happy, which had not happened in days, in seconds she had achieved it.

-Look I will not give more thought to the matter the thing is...

The sound of an incoming call to her cell phone interrupted my confession and she took the cell phone, talked for a few seconds with someone she told her that she would call him later because she was busy with something important which made me feel important again.

-Forgive me Eduardo for interrupting you, I had to answer to Valentin, had agreed to see him in the office to talk about Alejandra, I think he wants to go back with her.

That was the detonator of that bomb that momentarily went extinct but, in a heartbeat, it reacted, and all my courage and hatred reappeared, that energy that burned my skin.

-Going back to Ale never, I would kill him first.

-Since when you are so worried about Ale?

Her tone hinted that my concern seemed not to be friends but insinuating something else between Ale and me. That drop spilled the glass.

-Take this Becca, you can keep this, and all the lies poured there, look for another idiot.

- What are you talking about, Eduardo?

Her face was totally surprised, I did not expect a reaction like that and more the look of resentment that lavished on her.

-I know everything Becca, you betrayed me, how could you deceive me? The same imbecile Valentine told me. You want me to believe in your false promises, just tell me why?

Her face became reflective and taking her time thinking about what to answer.

-False? Just because I do not do everything you want. You changed Eduardo, since we returned to the city; you choke me at every moment

-Did I suffocate you? Do not say stupid things, everything I do in my life, every second of my time I am worrying and looking for a way to make you happy, that's what you call suffocating? Is it suffocating for you to love? Is that why you have to be easy with anyone? You are an idiot

-Asshole you do not understand that we are not teenagers, to be stuck always saying things corny is a waste of time. We are adults and we have too many responsibilities to waste hours trying to make you feel safe with the relationship. You look like a stupid child. You do not see the amount of stress and responsibility that I have in this project of the company that our parents founded, would you like all that to go to hell?

I never had heard her say some obscene word.

-And the fucking drug dealer that you slept with does not seem stupid? Or despicable Valentine? So, you can go there as a whore. I pity you Becca, or Alejandra who is like your sister, stealing her boyfriend.

-At least they behave like men and do not go whining after me like you do. You bore me with your same old crying, grow and mature Eduardo, and do not insult me again in your fucking life or I'll be your worst enemy.

Each of her words was a flamethrower burning my body, we did not realize that in each word we looked for lethal weapons to throw ourselves as if we were enemies, when we were one person in the past. My sandcastle where she was the most charming queen in the world fell apart.

-I never thought to hear that from you, I could have doubted anyone in the world except you, and all I did was love you. You have no idea how your words kill me.

-Love me? You just wanted to own me! Everything had to be when you said or wanted, always having to adapt to you and your ideas and your times. You wanted to dispose of me at your whim. Thinking that spoiling me would make me happy! But you spoiled yourself!

Everything you did for me was because you liked doing it. When did you do something that only I liked? When did you think "I will understand and if she cannot see me or be with me, I will not fight"? For everything you got angry, if things were not done at your whim, you fought. You are not the only man in the world Eduardo, and this does not revolve around you! You already told me that, I'm a whore, and that has not been any of your fucking business for months, you and I were no longer in a relationship.

I felt defeated, a battle that I did not have the strength to fight because I loved her too much and while my words only made her angry, she destroyed me more and more, and my eyes bled to tears until they were pale.

-The best thing is that we continue with our lives separated Eduardo, I cannot be with a child.

She immediately closed the door of her house leaving me no room for more words, although the only words I wanted to tell her even though my pride would kill me is that I wanted to continue with her that I did not care what she has done, the only thing that mattered was the relationship that we had for a lifetime. It's sad but it was the truth I died to be with her in spite of everything, and despite everything I still believed that something had driven her to do something that Becca, my Becca, had never done.

I came here trying to hate her but when I imagined my life without her, I realized that I could forgive everything for the immense love that I have for her, however I lost her forever.

I stopped over the sea and walked in the sand feeling the breeze trying in each inhalation to purify me and lessen my pain, but it was like a glass of water trying to put out a forest fire.

I walked a couple of hours without knowing what to do until I lay there on the cold sand in the dark wishing that everything was a horrible nightmare and the next day to wake up, she was by my side.

-Eduardo What do you want?

I knew that bar in the city very well, since I was a teenager I used to go there with my friends.

-Mezcal

-With ice? With soda? Sliced orange?

-Nothing, please.

I drank it as if it were water on a sunny day, feeling how the heat caused in my throat made me not feel that energy that made my veins burn.

-Give me another

The second created an effect of feeling a little stunned which helped me not to remember that immense pain, so I thought that was the solution to my problems.

-Give me another.

So, I drank until the place was about to close and I could barely stand up, it was still going through my head to get up with a horrible hangover but with her by my side.

-We are going to close Eduardo.

-Give me another mezcal.

-We are closing.

-The last one please.

I could barely speak. My gaze was lost looking at that table where we used to sit, the good that alcohol disguised the irritation of my eyes.

-I would not be your friend if I give you another mezcal, you can barely talk, and you have to drive to your house. Why do not you leave your car here and let Sara and I drive you to your house?

-If you give me a mezcal I accept, but if you don't give me another one what happens to me will be your responsibility.

-Ok, deal.

I convinced him to better call Luis to come and pick me. The next day I woke up with a horrible hangover, it was not a nightmare, she was not by my side, and I was lying on the bed looking to the ceiling asking God to tell me what to do, while tears were flowing from my eyes. I got up and poured myself a glass of mezcal that I had stored in the refrigerator and tried to lose my mind again so as not to think about her.

In order to be happy, we always think of love as synonymous with happiness, but it is not like that, love can cause the immense pain that I felt that night.

August 7, 2014

- Why did you kiss me?

-I do not know, I'm sorry, it was an impulse, I do not know, I've known you for years and you've always been by my side, at all times, good, bad, regular.

-I'm your friend; I always have been and always will be. We should not confuse that, now that thing with Becca is recent, maybe you feel alone and that's why you reacted like that, but I will help you overcome it, I will be your helping hand.

Although Alejandra tried to comfort Eduardo by making him believe that she would always be his friend, inside she had always wanted that kiss, which, although it was not with the intensity and love that she wanted, was incredibly nice for her. As a child she adored Eduardo, but he was always in love with Becca.

-Thanks, Alejandra, but I think we should try to be more than friends, we have known each other for a lifetime, we have spent so many good and bad things together that I think we know more each other than anyone else.

Once again Alejandra felt that her heart was beating a thousand times an hour and even though she thought about refusing to seek a thousand excuses, she knew that this opportunity was difficult, although in large part it was all because of the pain of the loss of Becca, it would not repeat itself. That's why she decided to take the opportunity she had always sought.

-We can try it, but always with the premise that if this does not work, we will continue being friends and we will be able to trust each other always, do you agree?

-I think it's excellent, why don't we go to dinner tonight at your favorite place and so we start with the right foot.

-It seems perfect; pick me up at eight o'clock at night in my house.

The evening was perfect, although Eduardo did not feel for Alejandra the same as for Becca, Alejandra was simply adorable, charming, and her personality would make anyone fall in love, her sweet way of expressing herself.

Sometimes it is necessary to experience what is unknown because it may be better, that happened to both of them when they left the restaurant and they were left alone in the living room of Alejandra's house and they made love. She was the second woman Eduardo was with and although it was difficult to compare the feeling of being with Becca, she liked him too much, Alejandra's dark skin was perfect and exciting. After that night, each day they felt more confident as a couple.

August 7, 2014

I felt just as obnoxious as Becca, trickster, fake, showing something that was not, but I was alone and Alejandra had always been my guardian angel, always taking care of me, watching me, what if I tried and did not work, we would still be inseparable friends, but if we took a chance and at some point I could feel even part of what I felt when kissing Becca, it would be the best thing that could happen to us, because as friends we understood each other, if we succeeded in time loving us would be perfect, apart from needing to forget Becca how it would happen, I did not mind doing anything to get her out of my life.

Why I dared to kiss Ale?

There are many reasons and perhaps most people judge me as opportunistic, abused or exploited.

The believers of perfect love will demonize me thinking that it was out of spite, I took advantage of knowing that Alejandra, although secretly she had always felt something for me since Luis once told me when we were in high school that Alejandra admired me in everything, I was the ideal man for her. At that time, I did not believe it but over time I was noticed that great affection she had towards me. Apart at that time I was in love with Becca's for my whole life.

Lovers of fair will condemn me thinking that I did it for revenge, walking away with Becca's best friend gave a context of seeking greater pain in her for having cheated on me. Also, for revenge may think of a dirty game to snatch Valentin before an imminent attempt to recover Ale.

Others will think that I kissed her because Alejandra, in the background, had always seemed to me a very attractive woman, apart from being adorable, she was charming but above all her voice could calm a war with every sound that came out of her lips. That's why her words were always a bomb in the worst moments of my life; she was the first to leave everything around to quickly drive to embrace me when she heard the terrible news of my parents' accident. I still remember it as if it were yesterday, she is getting out of her car addressing me at the moment when I had the phone in my hand, receiving that lack of news that she had previously known through the media. She did not even let me react negatively; she immediately hugged me and started saying such beautiful words from my parents and what they expected of me from that day that I felt an angelic calm of be with her.

I cannot fool myself, yes, I felt disgusted, yes, I was dying to take revenge on Becca, to see her writhe with courage for her mistake. Yes, I also like Alejandra, after Becca was the woman that attracted me most in life. Yes, her words and her love were indispensable to any other failure in life. I think it was the sum of all these feelings, but there was one stronger, one that by itself could tip the balance and compete with Becca.

That powerful factor was her love for me, and I do not mean the love we could have as a couple but that shown by her to see me happy even away from her, in the arms of Becca. That kind of love is not so easily found and was the one I needed, in fact I think it's the kind of nice love that anybody in the world wants, real love. That Alejandra had watched me be happy for years with Becca and enjoying every day of that happiness as if it were their own, that love that led her to always advise Becca the best to always maintain our relationship, even to keep her secrets. That love that everyone who talked with me wanted to see me immensely happy. That selfless love of Alejandra was what prompted me to touch her lips for the first time; I knew that if someone would always fight in her life to see me happy besides my parents and sister, it was her.

I could not let a love like that escape.

September 6, 2014

-How could you do that to my brother?

-Tere, excuse me, but that's between him and me.

-I do not give a fuck, Eduardo is my brother and he has always treated you like what you are not, like a lady.

- Stop insulting me, it's our relationship and nobody has to get involved in it, nor you, even if you're his sister, even if you're one of my best friends.

-I am no longer your friend, what you did to my brother has no name, we have spent a life together and you came to spoil everything.

-Why do not you complain to Alejandra? she was the one who brought that guy to our group. It was not me; I remember you.

The discussion rose in tone downtown the city, many people stared and listened to what those two beautiful women discussed.

-Alejandra just invited her boyfriend to the group, and you fucking took him for you. Bitch my brother loved you.

-Look Tere, I will not let you insult me, think what you like, you're right, we're not friends, have a good day, goodbye.

-Goodbye hypocrite, I hope I never see you again in my life.

-Don't worry, the least I want is to meet you again, ah! and do not even think about introducing me to your boyfriend, maybe what happened to Alejandra happens to you.

They said words they did not feel, deep down they had both always been together and sometimes they spent more time together than Becca and Alejandra, that's why they both said hurtful things, maybe more because of the fear of not being part of an informal family, which could have become it.

It was the straw that sealed the distancing of the five continents, since that day they never came together again.

Becca walked away with tears in her eyes, she knew that she had lost part of her family and all because of a stupidity that even she could not understand, but she had hurt Eduardo so much that she did not feel worthy to meet him again.

October 7, 2014.

I could never understand what I did wrong for her to forget me. That question assailed my mind every second and I could not think of anything other than that. I spent every second of my life thinking about how to pamper her, to take care of her more than me, to polish every floor she stepped on so that everywhere she went was ideal for her. So many sleepless nights, stressed by her problems, as if they were my own, sometimes crying because I could not help her feel better in each sad moment of her life. I walked hundreds of kilometers to be near her or to get the ideal gift for her. I wrote the deepest verses that came from my inspiration to shake her. I fulfilled every one of her whims up to the most crazy and eccentric, I made the worst ridicule of my life and I spent the greatest embarrassments, in order to fulfill each one of her desires that for me were orders, and I always fulfilled them, big mistake.

How could she leave me like that, just tell me she needed time, time?, if we had been together for so many years, what more time did she need to know that I was the man of her life, I did not need it, I never needed it to be completely sure she was the woman I wanted to be with until the last second of my existence.

What if I begged? I did it as I never had; I promised to change everything she wanted, to do what she said but not to abandon me. I cried, I implored, but everything was in vain, she was determined. Still several days later I looked for her thinking that ours had a solution, but it was in vain, her decision would not change.

I called her and I kept crying to her until that day when I discovered that she already had someone else, for so little she had changed me, she had changed the whole world that I put at her feet because of an idiot that appeared in her life.

Why?
Why? dammit.

It was so sad to stop enjoying her smile every day despite her bad mood and her mistreatment, I could take anything, endure anything so that she did not get away from me. But it was not my decision I would never have agreed to part with her.

March 21, 2015. Monterrey, Nuevo León.

I arrived at Dr. Alberto Kably's office, I had been skeptical about his treatment to stop drinking, but when I studied the results of his research and his method to eradicate abnormal behaviors, I considered it an excellent option. He was also influenced by the excellent chair taught by him to my sixth semester group. He was a brilliant teacher, not only had a wealth of knowledge in the study of the mind and human behavior, but also knew how to convey them in an excellent way because until now my group and I considered that in his subject was where we had learned the most about our career.

Therefore, my disbelief was not due to the proven ability of the doctor; on the contrary, I was sure that he was one of the best psychologists that existed, not only in Mexico but in the world. A little, my lack of confidence in the method was also due to the fact that for years I had heard that alcoholism is an incurable disease. So it happened to me, I tried unsuccessfully to end my problem by attending various support groups, Alcoholics Anonymous, yoga, the Twelve Step Club, religious talks, Christianity, hiking, meditation, therapy and, finally, I decided to try hypnosis, already disappointed to seek solutions, seeing the results achieved by this method, but above all by the expert who had opposite.

I remember that I started to drink more and more often when Becca left me, cheated on me with another, or with others, I did not want to find out anymore, my heart was shattered to know that she did not love me anymore, I felt that I just could live by getting drunk, feeling in a separate reality where thinking about her was not the most important thing, as it happened when I was sober.

-It's good that you made the decision to stop drinking, that step is essential to be able to make the hypnosis method work.

-I could not rest, all day long I had a headache from a previous hangover, sometimes for two or three days, I had a hard time concentrating on my activities to the point of forgetting to mention important things in a speech, I felt I was losing what I had left for alcohol.

-Indeed, alcohol is an addiction that also triggers many diseases and disorders, so I think you have made the best decision, and from this moment you will feel how you will improve your life without drinking.

- I hope doctor, although my pain in the heart is greater than any physical or mental suffering caused by alcohol.

- Do you suffer from a bad heart?

-No doctor, thank God no, but my girlfriend of years, Becca, has left me.

-Don't worry, time cures everything, except health, so you have to be fine by the time you get through this bad time.

-If it is that one day, I surpass it.

I believe that the doctor noticed me so distressed at that moment that he confessed to me about a new methodology developed by him.

-Look, next week, come around the office to check the progress of today's session and I will give you information about a method that I have developed to be able to erase unpleasant memories of your mind, completely.

- That sounds quite interesting, doctor, I wish I could pluck every memory in my mind where she appears.

- I have not yet tried the method in anyone, but I am almost sure that it is infallible, so, if you need it, with pleasure.

-Ok, doctor, I'll see you next week.

Glimpsing a possible hope of rebuilding my life made my day, not only thinking about forgetting her and being able to love someone else, but to feel cheerful again as it had always been, to walk around the office smiling, greeting everyone in the company and not having to arrive with a face of wake and from the greeting to the doorman at the first contact at the entrance of the company, it was depressing, and so on the cold walls of the elevator to find companions and in each open cubicle of the long corridor carpeted that led to my office on the top floor, had to say hello and pretend that nothing was wrong. Having to face long meetings and serve customers with a fake smile, the worst that has come out of my face. That was the most worrying thing, that's why those words of the doctor imagined in my mind all the positive changes, I would be the same leader from before and not a mechanical robot working to survive.

Attend even with co-workers and pretend that everything was fine. As on the birthday of that co-worker and a great friend of my father whom I knew as a child and his family, held in the largest hall of the company and pretend that I was happy trying to spend a pleasant moment when my gaze was fixed in the image of that cake with a fake automatic smile but my mind lost in the moment she left me. How heavy it is to smile when inside you do not want to know anything about life, and still undertake great projects and not always have the motivation to carry them out, not be able to convey that leadership that was often my strength to have great achievements working as a team , creating an important synergy that today was only the minimum effort and be all the time remembering those sad moments with that pain in the chest when images appeared in my mind of her deceit but above all the anxiety of wanting to run into her arms and not being able to do it.

My last project presentation had been a disaster, the hangover was killing my head and I could not think clearly, that's why I forgot several important cost details where I was an expert. I stumbled on some issues that I had been driving for years. And not to mention the use of psychology to maintain the attention of my public, that day I could not even keep for more than five minutes the attention of less than a dozen likely investors, not counting my appearance that was not the care of always, disheveled hair, badly cut nails, careless beard, tie with a single, very short knot, half-ironed pants, shirt stained with some coffee that I had drunk quickly before making the exposure to try wake up my mind. I even forgot my new business cards, I even had the old ones that I had in my portfolio for months and they were a bit damaged, that's why I had better obviate that part. When she was with me, I always got one hundred percent of the support of the investors, but in my last presentation only a third part chose to support the field for which I was responsible.

But Dr. Kably's explanation made me imagine an alternative, he made me think that there was life after her, but the most important thing was to think about the possibility that happiness existed without her.

March 28, 2015, Monterrey, Nuevo León

I traveled once again to Monterrey to attend the consultation with Dr. Kably and see the options I had for my problem.

-Pavlov managed in a simple way to condition a response on an animal, my method is a combination of several techniques and theories that consist of achieving an answer expected by my patient. In this case, the final response of the treatment will be that you are unable to recognize Becca or to remember any experience with her. I understand that is the goal of your interest in the treatment. Obviously, the effectiveness of the method depends only on each patient, in this case, the cooperation you do in each session and the strength of will for you to forget her, but above all of your voluntary decision to forget. In the first phase of the treatment we use a classic conditioning to try to divert those stimuli that make you remember her, towards something else, for example, when you see a rose, instead of feeling the emotion of that you gave her when you started your relationship in the beach, look, even just mentioning it now your eyes crystallized.

-I'm sorry, doctor.

-No Eduardo, you should not be ashamed of anything, on the contrary, the more sincere you are with me, the more I can help you eliminate every trace of her in your mind.

-That I will do, doctor, I promise.

-After some initial sessions in which we will try to condition those stimuli linked to her, we will pass to an operant conditioning, we will work on the answer, that is, on that feeling that you have so ingrained in your neurons, maybe even looking to focus on some other person or in some other object that can be the love of animals, to write, to nature, something that becomes as passionate as being close to her.

- Do you trust that it works? -Eduardo seemed to distrust any attempt to forget her since he had done everything possible to achieve it and, on the contrary, he missed her more every day.

-Who should trust and put all his faith in the treatment is you, Eduardo, remember that the most powerful thing we have is our mind and it depends on you feeling happy or unhappy, only it has that absolute power, so we must work hard to feed it positively and achieve your happiness.

-And is not some part of the treatment painful, doctor?

- Physically, impossible, you will not feel anything and emotionally, because I can tell you that in each session you will feel better, less emotional pain of having lost her, until it disappears completely, that is our indicator of treatment success, there are no average terms, you will be cured until you remember nothing about her, nor her name.

-And after the sessions, what should I do?

-Don't go ahead, we will go step by step, here the most important thing is that we have a scientific way of monitoring the successful functioning of each session. After working on the answer, and that this has its least impact on you, and that memory does not generate pain, we will do something that many have judged my method as unnecessary. Many thinks that just eliminating unwanted behavior is enough, but in the conditioning, there is something called "spontaneous recovery" and that is when the behaviors, after not having reinforcements or stimuli, are recovering from what had been managed to extinguish. For example, when I work with people with the habit of smoking tobacco, it is always possible, for many situations, to have a relapse or to recreate the same vices; in this case, it could happen that you come back to her and fall in love with her, because your feeling is very strong; She has all the characteristics of the perfect woman for you. We change many responses of sensations towards her, we do not change your personality, that would not be ethical, and I imagine that you do not want that either. Therefore, it follows that, if your personality fell in love with a woman with physical and emotional, cultural and spiritual characteristics, as there is likelihood that it will happen again, that's why we do as a last part of the method, hypnosis and a follow-up with exercises, if not daily, yes often during a month. The treatment works perfectly if you avoid having contact with the other party, not because you can remember something when you see her, in fact, you will not even recognize her, not even having her face less than a couple of centimeters; however, she may have some very strong memory of you or even some memory of you that you have returned to her, that is even stronger, against that we do not have any medicine, because it is programmed by you not by her and when you return it you gave her a weapon very strong so you can never forget it. With this technique we can achieve a deeper state of relaxation and a trance that allows us to eliminate that person from your mind. It is something that sounds quite complex, but with the conditioning achieved in the initial sessions it will be very easy to identify any memory very nested in your mind and it will only be a matter of ordering that unconscious mind to eliminate it, something like turning off all the switches of electric power, from each of the corridors of your house in a digital way, just by sliding the touch button of the switchboard on to off. Each hall is part of your life with her.

- Which would be the complications?

-None, the only risk would be that we did not succeed and you continue to suffer for her and even more, when you say that you have another relationship already stable, in which case I would return every cent invested in the treatment, in a few words the effectiveness of it is guaranteed. In the worst case, the treatment will only relieve your pain, forgiveness or you will forget about her. The only important thing you must do is to forget to make this work, the alcoholic cannot stop drinking but accepts that it is and a wish to stop being, the first step is the acceptance that you have a disease, in your case is mental called "fixation".

-That is the problem, I do not want to forget her, every day I dream of recovering her and when I do it while I sleep, I am the happiest man in the world, then I wake up and I see around me and she is not with me and probably never will be, It's like waking up with a horrible hangover after a night of unforgettable drunkenness. So I did not come here wanting to forget her, it is what I would least want in life, what I want is to alleviate this pain that eats me inside when I feel she's breathing near me, as well as when we slept together and when I realize that only it is a feeling created by my mind, I drink anything just to drink and I get stupid and I drive without stopping, I am a danger. The last time I woke up with a gun in my hand pointing at my head, lying on the bed, I'm sure that if I did not do that, it was because I could not overcame the dream of both drinking and sleeplessness, but otherwise I would not be here talking to you.

-I understand everything you feel and even more that is recent.

- Recent? I've been one year like this, feeling it like yesterday, do you think it's short?

-The time is relative child, if you want to feel better there is only one way I can help you, I know it is not easy, but you must accept it, you must accept that you lost her and you want with all your will power, forget her. The alcoholic refuses to accept his illness so he can not heal, the same happens in your case if you do not decide. If you do that, I promise you that I will do everything possible so that, if you ever cross paths with her anywhere, even one of your frequencies, you will not even know her name, nor will you recognize her face, she will go completely unnoticed to your eyes. You can remake your life.

-And how long does the treatment take?

-That is also relative, it can be a month, a year, a five-year period, that will determine how you respond to the treatment and your discipline in it, it may be that the classical conditioning is fast, in the operant, to disassociate your response, be slower and hypnosis is just routine, or it may be that in the three steps we take, it only depends on you, on the ingrained feelings and your memories, the behavior generated by each of them, of what so much interest and attitude you put in following each step. Each step will be very safe since I have implemented quantitative and qualitative methods to measure the result and most importantly, every month a test is carried out in which I observe what your prevailing memories are and based on that we can determine a percentage of progress in how much is what you no longer remember. Pure mathematics

- And what do I need to do to start with this treatment doctor?

-Only be completely determined to forget her, what you say and do not want to do is a vicious circle. It's as if you told me I want to get drunk, but not feel the bitter taste of a strong hangover. Here you have to be determined that from the moment we start the treatment you will forget her forever.

-Ok doctor, let's start now.

- No, son, you have to be completely sure of it, you cannot doubt for a moment, but nothing will serve all the time, money and effort you invest in your health.

-I'm determined doctor, so start please, tell me what the first step is to follow. -The decision of Eduardo not to forget her and look for some other alternative to not feel pain disappeared completely, on having understood that the problem had to be attacked at the root, although he did not like to do it, but when he made a decision he was disciplined in it.

-Ok, let's start then, I need you to make a list of all the objects and places that remind you of her, all of which you can remember until someday they stopped at a police station for infringing some traffic signal. You put the object or the memory, for example, the souvenir of a trip you made, to one side you put on a scale of one to ten how much it reminds you of her, and on the other side, it is the qualitative part, you put all the things associated with that memory that you have in the mind of first instance, for example, the price, the color, the day how it was, rainy, hot, she had short or long hair, black or brown. Describing both quantitatively and qualitatively each memory we can know how deep it is and in the deepest it is on which we work. The method has proven that, working with the strongest well-identified memories, small memories are automatically eliminated as by domino effect. Which is understandable, if you do not have a strong memory of your relationship, your mind will not even mistakenly open that drawer where the day was when you ate out-of-school chips. Therefore, this part is essential; it requires a lot of concentration. You have to take your time and do this exercise very rigorously with yourself, which is the foundation of the treatment, so I'm going to ask you to put yourself as comfortable as you can on this chair, if you like to lie down you can do it too, on the keyboard you are filling the format meticulously, I have a music player here, if you tell me what is your favorite song I can put it and that will help you concentrate on this task, you can cry even, we are in confidence, often happens, so do not feel bad that's what we need to know, which are the strongest, those that make you take inappropriate behaviors. The same music or songs that you choose can be part of those intangible objects that associate you with her. Take the time you want, and you can have some tea of your favorite flavor so that you relax and do not lose your concentration, the kitchen is by that door on the left. Anything I will be in the office next door serving more patients, but you can call my assistant with this device and she will let me know what you need. Do you want me to play some music?

-Yes, I was afraid to erase her, but the step to the abyss is given and there is no turning back.

- What song do you want to hear?

- "Missing you" by John Waite.

"Every time I think of you and always catch a breath" (every time I think of you I always hold my breath) that phrase was repeated like a drill in my mind and its notes made me able to resurrect each and every one of the memories of she, so I lay back and drank some wine, which we always drank when we celebrated any slight event.

And the first memory was that…

April 23, 2000. Coatzacoalcos, Veracruz

She was my dance partner in elementary school, I was surprised she remembered, she was the prettiest girl in the whole school, and I, even though I was her great friend, was someone who went unnoticed.

When they told us that we would dance and be assigned a couple, my first reaction was to think that the least I liked to do in the world was to dance and even less to make a fool of myself with a partner.

In alphabetical order the couples were chosen, first of all it was my turn, according to the list, to dance with Alejandra who was my best friend in elementary school, but that day she traveled, she did not attend because her parents had a serious mishap on the road that fortunately it only cost them some ribs and broken teeth.

I was worried that it was not her because I had all the confidence in the world around her, but when I remembered who was still on the list, even spilled the water that was drinking from the tap at that moment in the schoolyard, I was tormented.

Ethel, my pulsations began to rise, and my heartbeat accelerated to the maximum, just being close to she made me nervous and even more so that every year that passed her body was more of a woman than of a girl.

When I took her by the waist, I felt she was in heaven, she was taller than me and I looked tiny next to her.

- Do you know where my parents and yours want to travel this holiday?

Of course, I knew, among the five of us in a class recess we had thought of telling our parents that we wanted to get to know Europe, so it was almost a fact that that was destiny.

-I do not know, Ethel, do you know?

-Of course, we will do a tour through several countries in Europe, among which is what you and I have indicated as favorites, whenever we play world tourist, Holland.

-What good news.

Although the best news was that our parents kept coming together for everything and thus frequent us. Only when I was close to her, words did not flow as always, nonsense, my sense of humor worked, but even the jokes told bad when only she and I were talking.

That was one of the best days of my life because, from that moment, every day we talked because we had to rehearse for two months until the graduation party arrived. Contrary to what I thought, and it filled me with fear, when Alejandra returned to school, three days later, she was assigned as a partner to a classmate who had also been absent because of influenza.

From the fear of hearing the voice of the teacher of Natural Sciences says: "Martin Eduardo, your partner has already arrived, rehearse with her", to the joy of listening when she told Alejandra who her partner would be.

To be reluctant to dance, now, was the first to reach the center of the school yard to start practicing or better than that, when we delayed starting waiting for everyone to form in their position I could exchange some words with her, it was our moment alone.

That's how I recorded the day she turned years, April 18; her favorite color, the same as mine, the purple one; her favorite hobby, play tennis; she was fascinated by poetry; her favorite soccer team unfortunately different from mine, the Chivas of Guadalajara; what she liked to do most, cooking even if she was a bad cook and eating vanilla ice cream, just as I was fascinated by vanilla ice cream and all that was of that flavor; she confessed to me what her first name was, Rebecca, which did not please her very much because it reminded her of her annoying aunt who called herself equal, and who had put it on her, that's why she always asked the teachers to only mention her second first name.

Those two months served to talk about so many things and, above all, to feel more confident to be with her until I managed to make her laugh in all the rehearsals, with some nonsense. Even to the point of losing the nervousness of telling her some things that I would have died of pain before expressing them.

-What did you write in the Spanish class?

-A stanza of poetry

-Seriously? Show me.

-I feel ashamed!

-Why do you feel that way? We are friends, you should never be ashamed to show me something, you can always trust me.

Her words gave me the confidence to express what I could not have in a normal situation.

-It's that I did it for you.

She blushed, but in order not to distress me anymore, she asked me again.

-I would love to read it, please show it to me.

-Okay

"Your blond hair reminds me of the sun,

and your bright white smile to the moon,

that's why, after your steps I always go

admiring you as none. "

She finished reading it, her face reddened as I had never seen before and she embraced me tenderly.

I could not say anything else, when I tried to do it, I stuttered, so not to spoil the moment I kept quiet and took her by the waist and started practicing that day the dance, without saying a word until the next day.

April 18, 2015. Monterrey, Nuevo León

There are nights that are simply terrifying, sometimes for the pleasure of observing the full moon with all its immensity, sometimes by worry, the worry of not wanting to wake up and face a new destination, like a trip to an unknown and uncertain place.

I walked to Dr. Kably's office without hurry. Every block that walked in each piece that was missing to arrive, a memory appeared with her. I was assailed by doubt. I stopped. I stopped to think. Is what I was doing right? Otherwise I would regret it later. A few minutes later, I returned a few meters to have a coffee in the corner and continued walking. The meters that I needed to reach that bright spot in the office were eternal.

- Are you sure that's what you want, son? You did not seem very sure.

-Yes, doctor, what I most want in my life is to forget her, you have already shown me that with your combined conditioning method I can get anything that hurts me out of my mind. So, tell me what should I do to continue?

-You must come a couple of sessions or more for me to finish with the diagnosis, how deep that feeling is nested in your mind, for that we have to try some stimulus options and evaluate what the result is, something like go testing the effect of a medication on your body to finally do surgery that removes that pain, using the appropriate dose. In each session we apply certain simple stimuli and evaluate in the next if that is enough; otherwise, we perform another session, we apply other strong stimuli that are also useful to stimulate, and in the next session we evaluate the strength with which those memories are still stored in your mind. We use two options to verify that, one is to review point by point the questionnaire that you will fill me in these moments, and the other one is more sensorial, go measuring with electronic sensors the effect that still causes each memory. In this way we prepare your mind to get away from those thoughts.

-I did not understand anything you told me, but you do whatever it takes to make sure you I do not even remember her name.

- Are you sure you want to forget even that you know each other?

-Yes doctor, I do not want to know anything about her again.

-Ok, we'll do it; I'll leave you some tasks before the next session.

To work with classical conditioning, the doctor told me to gather all the memories I had of her and write them, it was the simplest way to find a link of associated responses.

With this, he sought to eliminate those tastes that I had and that were related to her, as was to each of the memories. A memory related to one of your favorite activities was potentially more complicated to eradicate.

October 27, 2015. Monterrey, Nuevo León

The mechanics to follow was to associate six very strong memories that he had with six activities that he liked a lot, the task was a bit complex, but at the time of achieving it one could effectively combat those memories by dissociating the feeling for them and indirectly by her.

Eduardo collected key chains from all over the world for which he had traveled; he also collected objects from some of those places. Another of his passions was reading. He loved reading novels and even more if they were romantic. From that habit he developed a taste for writing, any day, anywhere, in any situation, at any time, on a napkin, on newspaper, any blank space was an opportunity where he always wrote some beautiful stanza. Finally, he also liked very much to collect watches of all kinds, thus agglutinated with different extensible, colors, hands, and pieces from different parts of the world with different languagesand nuances, large sizes, small, fascinated by time and, above all, having it in his hand.

It was obvious to some extent, he could not associate the things that he liked to unpleasant situations, and in that case, he would stop appreciating the important things for him, such as reading. But if he related them to things that were not so important for them to become trivial, he would be able to diminish their effect. And so, it began, on the part of the memories of the world of poetry that he liked to write, of reading and of the collections he made, of watches and key rings. Associating them with non-important situations, with which, at a certain moment, he would not like it that much. And he would not remember her as the first part of the method, the phase of classical conditioning. In each session Eduardo was feeling a noticeable improvement, noticing how gradually by magic was disappearing from his mind his longing to do those activities that were once weakness, even liked but was no longer an obsession to do them frequently.

After three intense sessions of working on Eduardo's five favorite activities, there was no doubt that it was a great pain caused by his memories as they worked even overtime in the sessions, the doctor proceeded to do a test to evaluate how deep she was still in each one. This would allow him to know if his favorite activities were not so important for him, which could begin to disassociate the response related to his love for her and thus undertake the second part of the treatment.

The test yielded positive results; Eduardo was ready to move on to the next phase of treatment, the operant conditioning part. In this phase, he would try to work on the response of the feeling of love towards her, for which by means of valorizations with those same memories the Dr. would try to erase from his mind that sensation that each one had, taking advantage of the fact that its intensity had diminished, so they corroborated even the sensory studies carried out in his head.

He showed him the following objects:

A silver keychain with the letter "B", for Becca.

When he saw that silver metallic object, he remembered when Becca gave it to him one summer when she returned from a trip she made to Europe. However, collecting key rings was no longer a priority; even the keys of his car did not have any, contrary to the beginning of the treatment in which he carried three different key rings.

The indicators of his brain marked as this memory, one already very weak, did not cause great alterations.

A wooden rose whose parts, leaves, stem and set of petals were removable.

At the moment of observing that handicraft the indicators showed some high peaks, they showed an evident alteration, that was diminishing while he remembered that trip to Havana in which he gave her that rose and she returned it a few days later but engraved with her name to remember.

The doctor did not delve into this memory; he better noted it as one of his pending work to not remove other feelings.

A novel written by Alejo Carpentier.

He opened several of its pages in different chapters of the book to show the doctor some passages of the story he had dedicated to her. Although in each one he mentioned why he reminded her, sensory indicators did not show a great alteration, only in the final passage with a dramatic ending that Eduardo associated with their relationship, it was altered a bit but nothing compared to the indicators shown with the previous object.

When the doctor asked him if he kept reading frequently, he only said that he did not have much time to do it, which showed the effect or treatment on this type of stimuli.

A crumpled old paper napkin, apparently containing a message, opened it and was the verse of a poetry written in prose.

The doctor thought that by the nature of this memory would show the sensory indicators with greater alteration, but even that Eduardo loved poetry and that it was quite deep not only for the beauty and the passion with which he wrote it but for the moment so momentous when did. He wrote it the night they were together for the first time in Boca del Río. That's why it was written on a napkin, were the words and verses that came natural in that night that was extremely in love. He wrote it while she slept on his lap and showed it to her, but he did not give it to her, told her he would pass it clean to a word processor and print it every year.

But he kept the original in his own handwriting.

The doctor asked the same question with his penchant for writing and answered the same.

-I do not have time to do it.

A beautiful silver extendable watch with a black background on its dial.

The clock was the one that caused the most alteration in the sensory indexes, even in one of the peaks it was higher. It was his main hobby, collecting watches, and that was Becca's last gift, the last thing she lovingly bought for his last birthday before finishing the breakup. That's why it carried a great emotional load. But not with the levels of the wooden rose.

He made his notes on this memory and the points he found could work to achieve the disappearance of those peaks in the indicators.

And he recognized them all as memories he had of her, but he did not mention at any time that they were his favorite activities, for example, he no longer said that he collected watches or key rings, or that he loved to write poetry.

-Very good Eduardo, have you felt uncomfortable with the treatment? - evaluated Dr. Kably.

-No doctor, I feel very good. Each session I feel a great peace and makes me feel better every day, just suddenly happens to me in the session like todays that I have the feeling that I had already lived it.

-Yes, it is a psychological effect of the treatment to think that this is a déjà vu, but do not worry about it is a normal symptom observed frequently in the treatment.

The first step was taken, to get rid of every image in her mind of her.

November 30, 2015. Monterrey, Nuevo León

- Could you tell me what comes to mind when you see this? –Dr. Kably showed an old and ugly card that had some verses written on its back.

There were intense work sessions; in each one Eduardo was assigned a particular task. He had, from various relaxation exercises, yoga, walking outdoors, several options to try to clear his mind and look for other activities that he would like so much, like his greatest passion, to see Becca. And in that way, after numerous attempts, they were able to make the method effective. After two long months, the Dr. tried the final test of operant conditioning to see if he was ready to move on to the final part of hypnosis, with which he ended up with all those memories for the last time.

- No, doctor, I have no idea what that is, but it looks very old-fashioned; it must be from someone older.

Then he showed him a keychain with the letter "B" and asked him the same question again.

-I do not know doctor, is that mine? Or why do you ask? I do not know anyone from initial "B".

-No, it is not yours, a patient forgot it before you, but I wanted to see what perception someone had outside of certain objects, that in this case that patient caused a trauma his memory, for example, what do you say about this?

The doctor took from a very elegant marble-like stone box a wooden rose, whose parts, leaves, stem and set of petals were detachable. It was a nice detail and it made him shudder, but Eduardo did not imagine anything when he saw it.

-Well, it must be a nice detail of a boyfriend for his girlfriend or vice versa, it's a beautiful work of art, do you know where they sell them? It is a very beautiful gift.

-I do not know, I think that in Cuba, that was what the previous patient told me, that he bought it in one of his trips for the love of his life.

-I'm strange, I've never seen them, and I've traveled to Havana, doctor, I was studying a master's degree there.

-Then, I must have been wrong, maybe it was in Prague or Vienna, somewhere like that where there are very good artisans, where he had to buy it.

The doctor realized with these simple observations that the first phase of the treatment was working, so he continued with the test, disguised as a conversation between friends.

-And, what can you tell me about this? I think it was a very special gift from my previous patient for his ex-spouse, who died in an accident.

He extracted from the same marble box; a novel written by Alejo Carpentier.

-Well, he must have lived a very sad moment for the loss of his wife and also that he should have liked to read his ex-spouse a lot, but it would not make sense to give her something like that.

-Ha, ha, yes, don't you like Alejo Carpentier?

-I do not remember having read anything about him, I only know that he is a famous author in Cuba, I know because I was often in Havana and on one of those trips when I was studying the master's degree, I heard about that author.

He also unscreened from the box where the previous objects were, a crumpled and old paper napkin, apparently containing a message, opened it and showed it to me, it was the verse of a poetry written in prose.

"I started to feel quite annoyed at not being able to see her,

As if something between us had changed in an instant,

As if jokingly said little by little it was becoming a cruel reality.

Suddenly I felt like I did not know anything about her,

It bothered me not to have her eyes close,

I despaired if they spent hours and I had no notion of her life,

It began to worry me to feel that because more than something complicated,

It was impossible"

-It's very trivial, but I liked it, Doc.

-Trivial?

-Yes, very trite phrases, but with a forceful, totalitarian, deep end, I like it, you see that this kid must be in love, doctor. Not everyone writes something nice for a woman.

-While he is and do not imagine to what extent, has done anything to try not to hurt with her departure, with him I tried the method "Eradicate unwanted behavior" and boy has worked, he is much better.

-How pathetic, the day I'm like this, doctor, please shoot me.

-He, he, ok, I'll do that, he also left this-

- What is that? No!!! Do not tell me what I'm thinking? -the doctor sensed that he had recovered his memories with that strong detonator and felt that the effort of months had gone overboard.

- It's a story written for her! That guy must have been very much in love. - The doctor breathed again when he realized he had nothing to worry about; the treatment was going from strength to strength.

-He was; finally, tell me, what do you think of this?

He extracted from that box similar to those that keep fine cigars, a beautiful silver extendable watch, it was the last of the memories kept by the supposed former patient in love with a woman who no longer loved him, and apparently it was an anniversary memory for his watch collection. It was so beautiful that clock with black background and also silver hands that Eduardo even felt a great emotion just to see it.

- Do you like it?

-Yes, Doc. I love it.

February 23, 2016. Monterrey, Nuevo León

You walk slowly down that lonely path; nevertheless, you feel more accompanied than ever, the palm of a goldfinch is walking hand in hand with you, around you the damp green leaves of the imposing trees give shape to that path and give you a relaxing shade that covers you from the intense golden rays of the sun, the gray stones that form the path in all its shades dampened by raindrops, are also part of a pleasant company, you are not alone at any time there is always nature accompanying you, that gentle wind that numbs you.

You breathe deeply with each step you take, you feel how that air slowly enters and inflates your lungs until they become immense, it is the purest air you have ever felt, it even feels differently because you breathe with an incomparable softness and tranquility. Although the path is infinite, no part is the same, there are so many millions of combinations that make it unthinkable that some stretch of the path can only look a bit, just by varying the size of each element or its color to a greater or lesser degree landscape is unique, it is part of a more pleasant level for you. You see that because as you go one step further, although they are similar elements, each section is more appealing because of its color and the life of the place.

That route leads to the sea, and in the infinite you can see a beautiful blue sky, you enter the sea feeling how the water relaxes each one of your muscles that touch, the toes, the calves, the thighs, until it covers completely your torso, your back, your neck that make you feel relief and finally your head and each one of your hair are getting wet.

Contrary to what you have always experienced, when you are underwater in the sea, in the river or in a swimming pool, you do not feel that you lack oxygen, in fact, you do not even need to breathe, you can continue moving in the water to the bottom without pulling air from the surface or without using a tank with oxygen. It's incredible, but you can do it and you can dive deep into the immense turquoise blue sea.

The more you descend, the intensity of sunlight decreases, at that moment, when the light becomes dimmer you realize that it is your mind that vast ocean where you are submerging, so vast, where the whole story of your life fits , all your memories, all the learning you have gained over the years. As in any place, the oldest files are the most distant; your memories of past years are those that are in the depths, almost touching the sand.

You are looking for that memory, the mother memory, the one that made you create a permanent vision of her. You have to search deep to find it, it's not easy; it's like reaching a dangerous place and avoiding the dangers that are on the way. There are very painful memories along the way, which may even make you wake up when you feel the pain is unbearable, but you must endure as much as you can, stoically overcome any undesirable memory inserted there and that cannot be erased because it is part of your historical-cultural learning.

Your heart accelerates to see the memories of the past, the happy ones, but more with the painful ones, the loss of your grandparents, of your parents, the humiliations in the school, it is too strong to bear it but you endure to get to the place you want to reach , you have to resist, you must be very strong, endure whatever it takes to achieve your goal of achieving what was the first memory you have of her, suddenly, there are too many, in the clear snow, on the beach with an intense sun and her golden skin, in the rain kissing her, at school passing a math test, both nervous but confident to be close to each other, the breaks, from the first for any nonsense, to the final one that hurt like a dagger in the chest , the biggest pain you have ever suffered in my life, the heart is accelerating more and more, but you are aware that, as these years go by, your childhood is more about to be carried away and it will be easier to dig there.

You spend adolescence where your formal relationship began, then childhood and you are coming little by little to look for the moment you met her, perhaps that memory no longer exists, probably erased by existing such a wealth of information.

You remember the first year of elementary school when you sat together after a Mother's Day festival, eureka! That must be the first memory, but you cannot risk leaving there any that can contaminate your mind, you have to go to the depths to make sure that it is the first.

You search and only find happy moments next to your parents, when they took you to kindergarten, when they played with you, when they taught you how to play soccer, remember that kindergarten, it was called "Bambi".

Remember all those colors that you liked, the songs they taught you in classes, seem to be the oldest memories.

In that small court with two goals I tried to play what my father had taught me in the patio of my house, with my classmates, barely and we could kick that light ball designed for our age.

That ball came straight to me for me to put in that goal; however, I barely knew how to kick, I just remember that I closed my eyes and gave it with all my strength, I imagined those players of my father's favorite team and that when they scored goals everyone go crazy, and I turned it on just like I never had, with a huge force until I heard a very loud noise when I made contact with the ball, I opened my eyes imagining seeing the ball between those networks and all my team chanting my name like a true hero.

I saw it explode on the side of the goal, err by inches and slowly embedded in the chocolate ice cream of that girl of golden locks, who cried inconsolably before the amazement of comrades and rivals.

I ran immediately to apologize to her, I raised her face to tell her that I was sorry, it was her, that was the first time I saw her there squeezing in tears because of my stupidity, that was the first time we looked at each other and when she saw me she tried to stop crying as a sign of forgiveness and so that no one would notice, but at that age, a blow of those was impossible to avoid the pain and her sobs reached the ears of the director who happened to be there.

I stood in front of her hugging her a bit, trying not to notice, but it was useless, and they took me punished to the principal office.

While I waited standing in the corner to get my parents to talk to the authorities and tell them my feat, she entered without making a noise and gave me a candy palette, my God, what a beautiful smile, I had only seen her cry and I felt terrified, but seeing her smile made me know the world at that moment.

I found that moment thanks to God, now it was the doctor's turn to do his part and I pulled that last part of her that was left in my mind.

March 21, 2016

Eduardo had not seen Luis for so many years, since they stopped frequenting the five continents, and he really missed talking to him, he was always his best friend. They needed to catch up on much nonsense that they had pending. They always drank until they lost themselves since high school, Eduardo wanted him like a brother, they had spent so many things together, good, bad, sad, and regular, he went to meet him at the airport.

- You came to see Becca? - Luis told Eduardo when he got into his car.

- What Becca? - He started to laugh, and Eduardo had no idea why.

-Let's go, do not be strong, you should still miss her, for sure that's why you came and not because you wanted to see me. - Eduardo smiled as if following the game, but he had no idea what Luis was talking about.

-I do not know what you're talking about, but if you're playing fool to not pay me the bet of the final we beat your football team the America, it's not going to work you owe me a dinner in front of the boardwalk with a single malt whiskey 25 years old, have you forgotten?

-Ha, ha, ha, no, I do not forget.

A call just entered Luis's mobile phone.

-Luis, listen to me well, do not go mention anything to Eduardo about Becca, we had not told you because he has just come out of a treatment, he took to completely forget about her, erase her from his mind.

-Erase her, from where?

-I know it sounds amazing, but we'll talk when I see you, but please do not mention anything about Becca or her family, ok?

-Ok, Ale, do not worry, although it sounds half illogical what you tell me. – Luis hung up the phone.

-Now that you know where to go to pay your bet, tell me who is Becca.

-Nobody, I was joking to see if you fell into a bad joke, but I can never manage to trick you.

December 23, 2016. Coatzacoalcos, Veracruz

It was the most anticipated date of the year for Becca, just to see how the bougainvillea's turned their boring white color, to the magical lilac shown by the passage of winter, was the perfect occasion to radiate joy everywhere. But that day that beloved routine of many happy hours together the five, near the fireplace of the Hess Cavanhi mansion, telling anecdotes, drinking wine and cider, exchanging smiles and gifts, performing the most important ritual of Christmas Eve: placing baby Jesus in the manger of immense birth mounted by all members of the family in the vast and colorful garden.

That day her father arrived early from work, which surprised Becca; however, she was overcome by great emotion when she heard her parents talk about bringing them all together in the living room of the house. It seemed the prelude to a majestic Christmas Eve celebration. Becca, the eldest, was in charge of summoning her two brothers; Jaime was as always in the most distant room of the house enabled as a studio, where they had all the instruments of his band. There they spent hours rehearsing, his passion was music. It was not very complicated for him to be punctual to the appointment; he only had to fire his friends and colleagues from the musical group and cross the garden to get to the room.

Arturo was at his girlfriend's house, only three kilometers away, which took him a little longer to arrive.

The three anxiously awaited the news of where they would spend Christmas together, even Arturo thought of including in those plans his girlfriend Dolys, of who he was hopelessly in love.

Her father poured himself a glass of whiskey, so alone, into a small glass of cognac, gave it a big drink halfway up the glass and increased the vibrant emotion of each one, with every word that came from his lips.

-You know that you are the most important thing in the world for your mother and me, nothing and nobody can ever change that, we have spent so many Christmases together that just by hearing that word they come to my mind with a big smile in your faces immensely happy. However, some time ago your mother and I have had some problems in which you have nothing to do, but due to many circumstances we have decided to separate, to subsequently divorce irremediably, for which we wanted to gather you to give you the news and to say goodbye to you because at midnight I leave the city and I did not want to stop hugging you because of these dates.

A tear welled up in his face, nothing compared to the hundreds that Becca, Jaime and Arturo released. The claims were made by each of his children, but he remained stoic without uttering a single word and only embraced them for the last time, then went to his bedroom and packed his things.

The most illogical thing was that her mother also embraced him with great affection and even helped him pack his luggage.

What could have happened if they were like two best friends living together? As much as they tried to understand none of the three could accommodate the idea that, overnight, they took this sad decision, for a moment it crossed their mind to think it was a joke of bad taste, but it was not.

Before leaving, they once again tried with their faces swollen from crying to stop him, but it seemed something accomplished, it was not a problem of a day, and it had probably been this day, the result of hundreds of days of marital problems that the children would never understand.

That Christmas was the worst for Becca, the worst day of her life too, that date went from being the most longed for her, to a day she never wanted to live again. Enough reason to hate every Christmas detail from that moment. There would be no more Christmas Eve all together dining as a family.

That was perhaps the hardest blow in her life, and it came just when Eduardo was no longer there, the man who supported her as a child in every bitter swallow of her life.

She wished with all her strength a hug from him, but she knew it would be impossible to contact him again. She had lost him.

For Becca the separation of her parents was a breaking point, she had always seen them as the hope that in the end love always triumphs and with that separation she understood that love is not eternal and she lost the faith that one day Eduardo would forgive her . Her emotional stability that was already hanging by a thread was seriously affected because now she kept wondering if her parents had ever really loved each other and why her father abandoned them all after so many years being a happy family, she believed that all the moments of family love had been faked and that he really had never loved them. She was angry because she had believed in that farce for so long, she hated her parents for deceiving her and making her believe in eternal love, in happily ever after, those were just stories. She was destroyed because she would not know when she would see her father again and she wondered if there was another woman or if her mother was the one who had asked him to leave for another man. Until a day before this terrible news, her parents did everything together and happy. She did not know when the love died, did not know if they were only together for their children and that made her even more angry because then everything had been false, an invented story so that she and her brothers would not suffer. But she wished that even if it were a farce, everything would go back to normal, to wake up and see her father sitting in his pajamas having a coffee in the garden, wished she had more vacations together as a family, and wished that her father had never abandoned her. Her perfect family, her world has just finished being destroyed and Becca had no idea how to put all the broken pieces together. She did not know how to fix her heart that was shattered.

December 31, 2016. Coatzacoalcos, Veracruz

-Alejandra! Alejandra!

-Yes, tell me, I'm sorry, I was thinking about something else.

Alejandra had her eyes on the horizon, at that moment she was overwhelmed by two things and they had to do with the same person.

-Fuck with you, I can imagine who you were thinking about, Eduardo, my brother makes you stupid.

-It's not that, Tere, it's that I do not know how we're going to tell Becca the truth.

-The truth? what's wrong? You have nothing to be ashamed of, she threw Eduardo, left him for another, being that he loved her more than anything in the world, so we tell her and that's it, if she likes it, good and if not, too.

-I feel bad, she is my best friend, I should have told her about the relationship Eduardo, and I had started.

-Look, for the infinite ego that she has, I think that more pain will cause her to know that Eduardo erased her, supposedly from his mind, with that psychological treatment that he took.

- Supposedly? Do you think that he has not erased her completely?

-I'm not an expert on the subject, but in my very particular point of view it is impossible to erase all the memories from the mine, it is illogical, but hey, I do not know about those issues and I do not know if he deleted her or not completely what I can be sure that he does not love her anymore and he does not remember her at the moment, he only talks about you, so with that I am more than happy.

-I'm afraid of losing him.

-Fear, why?

-I'm sure; with the slightest memory of her he would run into her arms and I'll lose him forever.

-If it were like that, then it means that he has never belonged to you. So, you look for another guy and settled affair.

-For you it's very easy because you do not feel what I do for him, since we were children he has been close to me, I do not remember important moments of my life away from him, and the worst thing is that I do not remember me away from her as my best friend.

- Stop stressing, things that have not yet happened and probably will not happen, better concentrate on what we will say to her tonight.

- Shall we tell her? Please, Tere, I beg you, tell her, I would not have the courage.

-Look, the subject of the treatment with pleasure I tell her and believe me it will give me great pleasure to see her face and her ego thrown on the floor, will not bear to know that she has been forgotten, not because she cares about Eduardo, but because she likes to be the center of attention. But what about your relationship with him, there is no turning back, you have to tell her personally and if it is when you are alone, better that way, if you kill each other do not splash us with blood.

-How funny.

-It's a joke, but you must tell her, she must find out for you that you are her friend, for no one else. Besides, don't you remember she is going out with your ex when you still were dating yet. I do not know why you have so much consideration.

-Well, yes, but Valentin was a womanizer and surely used a thousand and one tricks to harass her.

-Well, think what you like, but I'll tell her that he erased her, and you'll tell her you're fucking her ex, ha ha ha.

-Ok, but do not leave me alone all night please, I'm afraid she'll look for Eduardo and I'll lose him.

-Don't worry, I'll be watching you all night and I'll take you drunk to your house in case we have to drown the pain as always, as a true friend does, we'll start the year drinking.

January 1, 2017

Every second of her life; happy, sad, ecstatic; It passed through her mind in a fleeting way. Never thought to live that moment, if something had been safe in her life is that Eduardo would always love her, would always be there for her.

Someone had to give her the cruel news that it would hurt not only her heart, that she had only loved Eduardo in her life, but also her ego and her vanity as the perfect woman that was always for him, and for everyone who knew her and remained in love of her beauty.

After midnight, as they celebrated the New Year, after the ritual of the grapes, the cider, the suitcases. She felt the need to talk to Eduardo, but he had changed his number, so she decided to ask those who knew where to find him at that moment.

-We have to talk to you, Tere and me.

- What's up, Alejandra? You scare me, did something happen to Eduardo?

-No, thank God no, or good yes, but it's okay, healthy, the problem is another, I would say emotional. - Alejandra took a sip of the glass of tequila she was carrying, of the nervousness she felt at revealing the truth to her.

- Emotional, what's wrong? Explain to me please, you are terrifying me.

-Look Becca, we must talk about the decisions Eduardo has taken in his life for a while

-Ah, is that it? Now he has messengers to do him the favor of telling me what he does not have the pants to do. Don't he love me, come and show it, be like a man and fight for the love of the woman of your dreams as he told me on thousands of occasions that I was. - Becca was already carrying some wine glasses and that made her lose control of the conversation a little.

-No Becca, this is serious, look, you know that you broke up a while ago and that to him it broke his heart, more after seeing you with Valentine, and that it is clear that I did not care about Valentin anymore so do not feel bad, then I think he also learned about other things about your sponsor of the foundation and well, so as not to make a long story, it was a blow too hard for him, he got lost in alcohol, he became an alcoholic, he was on the verge of falling into drugs, but fortunately one of his teachers from the university helped him through hypnosis to overcome his alcoholism and any anxiety about another addiction. He also showed him a treatment he had developed to eliminate tragic or sad memories in people, to overcome any trauma. And then apparently, decided to eliminate you from his memories.

- What?! Did he erase me from his mind? - She released a sarcastic smile mocking what they were trying to tell her, thinking it was absurd. -As in the movie of "Eternal sunshine of a spotless mind", but only you can believe in those fantasies, it is fiction.

-Well, let's say yes, in fact, if he sees you, he will not recognize you or your family, so we wanted to ask you to help us support him, not look for him and explain to your family what happened in case they see him and do not greet him. Our parents have always been great friends, so we want to ask you to help us. Please Becca, he did not want to suffer anymore, it's more, you already have another relationship so the best will be...

-I do not have anything; Eduardo is the love of my life, always has been. - The tone of her voice turned into one of courage. A flow of tears began to run down her face, apparently that news hurt her more than what Tere and Alejandra had predicted. They were so surprised by her reaction that they both got up from their chair and came over to hug her and comfort her.

She cried with a feeling that showed how much she adored Eduardo, but why she had done everything she did.

-If you love him, you must support him to get ahead, he invested his time and all his effort so that the treatment could be effective, he was even on the verge of committing suicide on one occasion for you, that is why we all advise him that the best thing was to forget you and what better if he could do it scientifically, tested.

A few moments passed when she stops crying and felt a great courage, until she calmed down a bit.

-Ok, I will try, although I do not know how hard it is, he was by my side all my life always supporting me, but if he made that decision, instead of acting like a man and faced me or looked for me to win me back, ok, I will not look for him, if he wants to be the coward who flees in this story, go ahead.

-There is another thing I have to tell you. – Alejandra said while taking Becca's hands.

-Now what? Are you going to ask me to quit my job, so I do not see him at the office? - Becca answered very reluctantly

-No Rebecca, listen to Ale. - Tere asked

-I'm all ears, I just clarified that I'm not going to give up anything in my life because of the stupid and coward Eduardo.

-Becca I'll get to the point; Eduardo and I have started a relationship. -Alejandra said directly and Becca froze, her mind could not accept what she was hearing.

-Relationship? But if you've always been friends, it's not like you're just starting that friendship.

-We are a couple. - Alejandra clarified and, in that moment, Becca let go of her hands.

-How could you? - She said threateningly

-I have always loved him and he wants to be happy, I make him happy Becca. As your friend, I had to tell you.

-Friend? You are an opportunist. You take advantage of that he does not remember me to get close to him and surely copies all my details with him to make him fall in love with you.

-I'm always going to be your friend Becca, even though you were the first one who got involved with my ex. - Alejandra demanded indignantly for the words of Becca and for the guilty that felt to know that those words were a little certain.

-You're so stupid to believe that I, Becca Hess, would have something with someone like Valentine, I'm not you that are satisfied with so little. And since we are being honest, I clarify that he kissed me by mistake and that from that moment between us there has never been any contact of that kind. But of course, someone as insignificant as you believe that a woman like me would stoop to be with a man like Valentine.

-Do not offend Alejandra, you cheated on my brother. If it was not with Valentin, then with the gangster who followed you so much. - Tere intervened to defend Ale.

- Look Teresa, if I only address you the word is for education, some time ago you and I made it clear that we are not friends. So, I'll tell you this once and I hope your brain so small understands it. Number one, your brother and I had been separate months when that happened, and it was not cheating. And number two since you are being so honest when the two have not even said hello to me for months, if you had been my friends you would have known that what happened with the gangster was against my will and that I was unconscious.

- They are lies you tell for us to forgive you. - Tere whispered with a lot of indignation, while Alejandra watched Becca and knew that she was not lying. She felt even guiltier because Eduardo's hatred for Becca did not have strong foundations, if he knew what had really happened, he would have supported and forgiven her. Alejandra wanted to tell Eduardo the truth, but her heart refused that idea, she could not lose him now that she already had him with her. She justified herself by thinking that for Eduardo's mind it would be too traumatic to remember so many forgotten memories, it could affect his health.

-For you to forgive me. I'm not interested in her forgiveness, let alone your friendship. I do not need to lie, after all I had lost everything months ago, if I wanted to flee the forgiveness of someone was Eduardo's but apparently, he is a coward that is satisfied with so little. - By saying this she pointed to Alejandra

-Becca, I'm sorry. You will always be my best friend. - Ale said in a calm tone trying to find peace.

-You were always in love with my boyfriend, and that does not make you a best friend. As soon as there were problems between us, you approached him without thinking about my feelings, and that does not make you a best friend.

-Forgive me please. - Alejandra pleaded

-No Alejandra, never. I will hate you until the day I die. And you will remember me for the rest of your life, in every moment that you are with Eduardo, you will know that I will always be the great love of his life; that at any moment I can decide to approach him, remind him of our love and snatch him away from you. He will never feel for you even half of what he feels for me and that will chase you like a ghost for the rest of your life. You are the consolation prize, nothing more. I pity you; you settle for so little. So do not forget this, Eduardo could erase me from his mind, but I'm still in his heart and you'll see it every time he kisses you or hug you or have sex, he will never love you.

With that Becca went away and left that party, with her head held high because she was Becca Hess, and nobody would see her defeated or humiliated. Alejandra's betrayal had broken her, but she would not show it to anyone. She got into her car and drove home crying. Eduardo and Alejandra had betrayed her in the worst possible way, she hated them with all her being; and despite that hatred she knew that they were never going to be really happy because she would always be in the middle of them and she smiled.

At that time she dried her tears and her pride and vanity were more than the pain he felt and he took it as an affront, so she went to her house to destroy everything, with blows, what had to do with Eduardo, her room seemed a battlefield with so many broken memories around. She kept them in a garbage bag and left them outside her house and endured several nights crying with anger, thinking that one day he would regret and who would cry, it would be him.

March 21, 2017, Coatzacoalcos Veracruz.

It was the first day of Becca's work away from Eduardo, she had decided to change her office to another part of the city so as not to coincide on any occasion with him, or what was worse with him and Alejandra together or embraced, that image only of seeing it in her imagination was the most painful thing she had ever seen in her life. Seeing it with her own eyes seemed inadmissible. This is why she moved her entire team to a new suburb, quieter, less tormenting for someone who wants a distraction so as not to think once more about what she considered the highest treason.

She still did not understand how her best friend could snatch Eduardo away from her, but especially how he could have even thought of another woman other than her.

It was the daily thought as she drank that coffee lean looking through the window of that last floor where her office was, which not only warmed her hands on that day that was cloudy with a cool wind, normal in March because in March the usual is an unusual climate. She also warmed her thoughts, for instants she thought of a revenge, but then she calmed down, she would never hurt who had been her partner for almost 30 years, the happiest of her life, or her former best friend who at one time was like her sister, with whom she lived so many crazy things and made so many trips, were accomplices of so many secrets that in spite of everything they still kept for loyalty, they would never use.

At times she thought about changing city, even country, had the necessary pretext to do so, was the leader of a project of global impact on the part of the company.

Also at times she justified that betrayal by remembering that she had also had a great responsibility, she stopped frequenting Eduardo, but especially in what seemed inexplicable, how it was that in a moment she felt that she no longer loved him, if he was all for she. The university stage away from him for the first time in her life, made her live different things in life that she did not know, she felt free, but, free of what? Of Eduardo? Today all she wanted was to be held in his arms and never escape them. Nobody values what they have until they see it lost, that proverb went through her mind every day.

It became an unpleasant routine, after drinking coffee very early in her office with that panoramic view of the city from the window, having all those thoughts of sadness for not having him, betrayal of her friends, and nostalgia for memories.

Sometimes she saw, when the clouds allowed it, that imposing building of the company where they were both practically born, and some tears sprang up. She did not imagine having Eduardo face to face and that he acted like a stranger, when both knew even the most intimate parts of the other, their weak points, both in the body to provoke pleasure, and emotionally to generate pain. They knew in advance when they were in a situation or problem, what would be the solution that each one would give, only Eduardo knew Becca's fears, and Becca knew everything that Eduardo was passionate about. For that reason she felt calmer and more distant, it would be unbearable to see him and not ask him if with Alejandra he spent moments when he could feel immensely happy to tell her that he would never think of anyone but her as he did with her.

Apart from changing office, phone number, social network accounts, helped Valentin and Leobardo knew nothing of her existence. And so, she became accustomed to each of the paths that led to her office and to all the events and places that were in that new context, in that small community.

However, that ritual was every day when she drank that cup of fresh coffee in the morning when it was barely dawn because she was the first to arrive at work, because she sometimes could not sleep because of the torment of imagining Alejandra and Eduardo together. Sometimes at 4 o'clock in the morning she would get up, to recover from those nightmares, run around the park in front of her house, for an hour, then shower and arrive at the office in five minutes. Maybe she had not detected that drinking coffee was part of that classic conditioning that she had done for more than a decade with him. That stimulus involuntarily and immediately awoke all memories of him, from the strongest as that Christmas in Chihuahua in the mountains or just a normal day at home.

She thought about that a few months later when she searched the internet about Dr. Kably and his research to find out what had happened to Eduardo. It was a Sunday with nothing to do in her house other than to torment her mind, she decided to be productive and investigate. She read about his treatment to erase memories, but above all when she read about Pavlov's classic conditioning and immediately came to mind the daily cup of coffee, that was perhaps one of the few stimuli that she had attached to him.

From that moment on, she tried to be self-taught about everything she had read in each of the articles available on the web, Eduardo had a very expensive treatment to forget, which she could try without help from anyone. She arrived at her office, opened the wooden door where she kept all the cups and threw them in the trash, she did the same process with the bags of coffee from all over the world that she had kept in a showcase and that adorned a part of the place, it hurt to do that on a very early Monday, however the most painful was to feel the addiction in her body for caffeine and not being able to drink it, she was sure that if she had kept a bag, she would have overcome the temptation, so she made sure there was no coffee nearby. She bought a speaker to put at all volumes a type of music that had a great rhythm and that was not to Eduardo's liking. It was not complicated, the reggaeton fulfilled those two characteristics, so every day she put that music at full volume and start to work. She was sure that Eduardo loved her more than she loved him, so it would not be hard to forget him. As if there were magic formulas or cooking recipes to forget.

Loving can become a chronic disease.

December 24, 2017. Coatzacoalcos, Veracruz.

I laughed like a fool in the middle of that restaurant where I had breakfast that Christmas Eve.

I read that ad again and laughed again, drawing the attention of the diners around. They looked strange to me like I was crazy. Crazy the guy who came up with that idea and put that ad in the newspaper of the most local circulation.

I turned to see the beautiful girl sitting at the table next to mine and I opened the page completely and showed it to her.

- Who publishes this? It must be a joke.

She also laughed aloud when she saw that unfolding and I was no longer the only idiot laughing for no apparent reason.

A large image of that character, symbol for many generations like the enemy of Christmas, the famous green doll named Grinch. He announced a great party that night at a hall of events for all those who hated that festival; there would be a DJ with all kinds of music except Christmas and a buffet with all kinds of food except the traditional Christmas Eve. It was like a cult party invented by my countrymen. Apparently, someone had had a bit of creativity and designed a nice party for those of us who are not fans of this party. How big would be the segment of deranged people like me, hating Christmas in silence for apparent reasons. There would only be one way to know. I could not stay with curiosity and I just called to know details.

-Excuse me, what's included in the Christmas-hater package?

-Includes the dinner and drink that you like, until one in the morning, we guarantee that there will not be the smallest detail related to Christmas. In Coatza Enterprises we are aware that not everyone is the same; there are successful people who do not like these traditional and monotonous parties.

I fell in love with that idea when listening to the salesgirl explain the theme of the party. I had no intention of going to that celebration, but when I heard that simple but forceful explanation, I had no other choice.

-Reserve me a place, can I go alone?

-The majority of the attendees that we have already confirmed attend alone sir, that feeling that you have is also shared by a select group of people, who know how to discern what to do on a holiday, take advantage of it with a good wine, the music that you like and away from the Christmas embarrassment.

Now I was more than convinced, after that precise observation made me lose the fear of attending.

- At what time do I have to arrive?

-We opened at seven o'clock in the evening; we recommend that you arrive at that time so that you can make the most of everything we have prepared for you.

I arrived at the stipulated place; Boulevard Beach number 127. The clock just pointed seven with seven minutes. There were already several vehicles parked outside, apparently had a great demand this celebration, the first of its kind in this city and the first in the world that I knew well. And proudly it was in Coatza.

-Excuse me, I have a reservation on behalf of...

- No! Do not tell me your name, just your reservation number.

-It's 724.

-Ok, with that is enough, here we will assign a name that you will use while you are here; nobody will know your true identity.

- So, we will all use a different name.

-So it is sir, you enjoy the night without inhibitions, nobody knows you and nobody knows your name, you can even wear a mask which is optional, forget your problems, today you are just a man partying, we celebrate like any another day.

I loved the idea, so I went in immediately, at first I thought it was nonsense that mechanism to change your name, but the truth is that that trifle made me feel much more in confidence, I even went in dancing, motivated by the party, I never do.

The tables were at sixty percent capacity according to my assessment. I served a craft beer made right there, which was named after the city "Coatzacoalcos". It was dark and although it did not taste so exquisite, the excitement of being celebrating a day like this and in a different way, made me think that flavor was better than a London Pride beer.

I sat at the bar to drink while dinner started.

     - Are you free to tell me your anecdote of hatred for Christmas?

A beautiful woman approached the bar and made me smile with her questioning. At another time it would have bothered me, but at the moment I had overcome it and I was very happy.

- Anecdote? There's nothing interesting to tell, better tell me, I stared at the badge she wore with her nickname.

- Prude queen.

We both laughed at the nickname she had been assigned for the night.

-And you are?

I had my badge turned over and at that moment I put it in the correct way.

-Elvis Bowie.

We both laughed so much; it is assumed that when entering your personal data and some of your tastes, the computer randomly chose a name of any quality or even up to your age.

-Well, Elvis, notice that until a couple of years ago this was the most awaited date for me, the ideal moment to unite the whole family, those moments that are forever engraved in the memory as the most joyful and nostalgic. But last year my father joined us all in the living room of the house to give us the terrible news that he was going to divorce my mother, which made my life completely turn upside down and go from being the most awaited date for me in the year, to one that I never want to arrive. What about you? To what do we owe your income to this select club of haters?

-Something similar to your case, it has to do with my parents, year after year I also longed for this date to spend time with them and feel in full confidence, as when I was a child and was totally protected and happy near them. They did not divorce, they just left me, they disappeared a rainy night in a plane crash and from that moment on Christmas was never the same again. This day I only have fateful memories, until this moment when I'm chatting on Christmas Eve with the most beautiful girl around. - She blushed a little for the compliment thrown and a tear slipped from her cheek, it seemed that my short story had made her feel sad, and it was not for less, it was the first time I told it and I did not cry wildly. I dried her tears with my handkerchief that I always carry in my pants pocket, as my father taught me.

- Do you have a girlfriend?

I did not know what to say, I could not deny Ale with whom I was engaged, but it crossed my mind to do so, after all, probably the next day no one would remember what happened at this party. And so, I tried, denying her, but she disarmed me.

-If you think so much, it is because someone must exist. - I betrayed myself and I was exposed.

-It is complicated, but yes, I have a recent relationship not so formal. - Recent? I had decades of knowing her, not so formal. Yes, we were already engaged. But I think I came out well when I changed the conversation. -And your boyfriend? Such an incredibly charming woman could never be alone. -She felt uncomfortable with the question, I noticed it because she changed her face that looked cheerful, when I was questioning, to a stern one when I launched that questioning.

-My first boyfriend will always be my greatest love; the problem is that he is no longer with me.

She became too sad for the loss of her great love that I better started talking about other topics to distract her.

Time flew by telling us so many things and laughing like idiots. We chatted for a while, it was beautiful, I remember ever having had a dream of a girl like that, with those characteristics so beautiful in all senses, physical and emotional.

We dined accompanied by large candles placed in the center of our table and at twelve we did not know what to do, we stared at each other until she broke the silence.

- Happy day we met! -These words stuck in my heart and in my mind, indeed that day could stop being an unexpected date, for one where I met an unforgettable woman and, one never knows, maybe someone very important in my life.

-It's true, today we fulfill one day of that.

We both laugh out loud.

As it was a dance for all the DJ was playing, obviously in electronic version, the songs requested by the audience, when he approached us she said something in his ear, I imagine the name of some song, but I could not hear what it was .

- What song did you order?

-You'll know, right now you're going to dance with me.

-Dance? You do not know me beautiful, I do not dance nor having two extra feet.

-Will you reject an abandoned woman on Christmas Eve?

She took me by my hand making a bow as in ancient times when a gentleman invited a beautiful lady to dance, the moment the DJ started to play that commercial Aleks Syntek song. She took me by my waist to dance in the old style, glued and hugged; I loved taking her waist strong in my arms.

Who would choose that song for a night out on Christmas Eve? well, it was excellent because what we least celebrated was that, then any song like that, however stupid or ugly it was, was ideal for building new memories.

"A small part of you is enough for me,

To be the happiest man,

Just to have you here with me,

I can feel love just like that. "

She brought her lips so close that I could not resist trying to touch them, but when I tried, she moved slowly back, damn it! I fell in her game.

I wished that song would never end; I felt her body fit perfectly in my arms as if we had been dancing together for years, which in me would be centuries, because I danced very little.

And that techno ballad converted into an electronic version came to an end. I thought I would never say those words in my life, I do not remember doing it with someone.

        - Do we dance another? - She was also surprised at my proposal but nodded and we returned to the center of the dance floor.

        -I would love to, but now you choose one song.

-It will be much better than that commercial ballad chosen by you prude queen.

-Are you sure? - What do you want to bet? It will be so commercial and cheesy that I could guess it.

-If you guess, I spend the rest of my life with you. - I thought to myself, she would never hit a song that I used to listen to, it was not the commercial classics, moreover, when I was a teenager my friends told me that I listened music for gays, which resulted in a future being music ahead of their time.

I approached the DJ and asked him strongly, not without taking a whiskey on the rocks as I saw he was drinking from the beginning, playing the song I had chosen to dance with her. That guy was a genius, a song he did not have, he would download it from a player and then mix it. It was incredible to hear everything that his hands let flow.

I returned to the dance floor, it was about to finish the current song, which we did not like either of us, it was reggaeton, and she gave me the napkin with which she cleaned a little lipstick that had run with her drink.

-Can you leave it on the table?

I took it quickly so as not to lose a second in case our song started, and I left it on the table under my beer.

- Do you know that song? - Everyone danced loose, and we were still holding each other closely.

-No, but it sounds very tender.

Her response seemed natural, but it was suspicious that the name of that song was that word and more with that ironic smile that she did when she was joking.

The music ended and now I reached to touch her lips for a second and moved by pulling my arm to the table to take her glass of wine and toast with my vulgar bottle of dark beer.

-Look!

She took the napkin still attached to my bottle, removed it and opened it showing me a word that made me shudder.

"Tenderness"

- It cannot be! How did you know? Did the DJ tell you right?

She put her fingers in my mouth to shut me up.

-Let's dance one last before leaving.

-Of course. - The party was about to end and I was dying to go to the boardwalk to see the Christmas sunrise with her, to write a new story, I did it so many times that I wanted to feel the emotion of seeing the first rays of the sun on the sea , with all the unequaled nuances that she takes, with her, only with her.

-Which one do we choose?

-I'll choose it, you will like it, I am sure, it is more, it will make you cry.

-Ha, ha, ha, impossible, and less now that I'm so happy here with you, if it makes me cry, I promise to play it on the day of our wedding as our first dance.

-Ha, ha, wedding? What did I miss? We are already getting married and we hardly knew each other, but well you said, that will be the waltz of your wedding if you cry, is it with me or with the lucky one who is next to you at the isle.

She took me once more by the hand took me to the dance floor and we began to dance that strange song and suddenly a couple of minutes after nothing without feeling it, without knowing why my eyes slipped a couple of tears.

I did not know what to say or what to do, she dried those tears with her hands tenderly and then mocked tenderly too, that song made me shudder, I knew it well, it was Major Tom.

- So, you don't cry man of steel?

I did not have any more words until the song ended and just at the moment, we were taking our things and she had agreed to see the sunrise with me, a call came to my mobile phone. I went to the bathroom to hide.

-Ale, how are you?

-Happy Christmas, my love, how are you? What are you doing?

- Me? Here drinking a beer in a bar and you? - I stammered a little at the nervousness of her noticing.

- Arriving in Coatza, I came driving from nine at night from Veracruz after having dinner with my parents to be with you in this moment, I could not leave you alone.

If ever in my life I felt that I thought it was stupid and I used to hear in women that "I'm confused", at that time it was, I was confused, the night had been magical, but the detail of Alejandra abandoning her family and her Christmas dinner to run to see me on a very sad date for me, made my skin crawl.

She noticed that I was phoning near the toilets and she just smiled at me.

-The car is about to become a pumpkin.

Her joke did more than laugh, I felt sunk in a deep black abyss, I did not know what to do or what words to say to not spoil what had been perfect hours by her side, I could say anything, but lie to her.

-It was my girlfriend; she just arrived in the city, drove at night and left her family to come see me.

-The rod is set very high, impossible to overcome that, how lucky you are dude.

She came over and gave me a pretty tender kiss on the lips.

I tried to say something, but again she trailed my lips with her fingers and walked away quickly.

When I tried to go out and look for her, even though it was only a few seconds, I did not reach her anymore; I looked for all the cardinal points and nothing. She vanished, literally. And I screamed like crazy in pain, heartbreakingly.

December 24, 2017

That morning I decided to buy the newspaper, with the current technological advance I preferred to read the news online and not complicate me to go every day to a post to buy a copy of that gray paper that smelled strange and stained hands. On that occasion something forced me to buy that newspaper.

Right away, the Grinch's face caught my attention; it had always been my favorite character at Christmas time because for me it represented the hope of changing, of beginning again, of the power of faith. Then, I read the ad and laughed, I felt so identified with that nonsense, a Christmas party for those who hated that holiday, I immediately dialed and booked a place for myself.

I remember that Christmas was always my favorite time of the year, the smell of the tree pervading every space of the house, the thousands of lights that were reflected in the shiny spheres and obviously receiving gifts. It was always my favorite time until I left him. Now, the longing for his presence, the desire to go shopping to find the perfect gift, the desire to share with him the birth of Jesus, made this day unbearable, missed him more than ever. Then came the divorce of my parents and it became an ordeal that December came for that sad memory.

That afternoon I started to get ready and decided on a black dress, I felt mourning, black was the least Christmas color of all and for a moment it crossed my mind to wear my old Grinch pajamas, but I considered that as Coatza is a small city, I would meet someone, even if I was an acquaintance at that party and I did not want to take my anti-Christmas cynicism to the extreme of being the talk of the city the next day. In addition to that I did not want to see my image turned into some meme and that circulated through social networks, making my life more unbearable than it already was.

I drove carefully to that room located on the coastal boardwalk, I saw vehicles passing by with families who were singing merrily Christmas carols and I felt frustrated, why was everyone so happy? Christmas was overrated. I went up the window of my car and I put one of my favorite songs and that I once dedicated him "Million reasons" by Lady Gaga, this time I was the one who sang at the top of my lungs and some tears ran down my cheeks, I did not try not to feel miserable, what if I cried or not, this day I did not have to pretend a smile and make stupid jokes, this day was for me and my pain.

I parked near the entrance, there were not many cars yet and I took the makeup out of my purse, it was one thing to feel depressed and quite another was to look like a crazy woman that just got out of the asylum, so I touched up my eyes that were still red, but at least the eyeliner was no longer running and I looked presentable.

I got out of the car without hurry, I adjusted my dress because I never liked to show more and when I looked up, my world stopped, I felt my heart beating a thousand times an hour while my lungs seemed to have stopped working by printing. There, a few meters away from me, was he, the love of my life, parking that white van that I knew by heart and could easily recognize in the distance, just in spite of everything, he was everything to me.

I recharged myself from my car trying to calm down so as not to be stupid, in my mind I debated whether to stay or leave immediately, I was very confused. But I believed blindly in the signs that life gives us and I knew that the need I felt that morning to buy the newspaper and the impression that the announcement of that party had caused me was a sign that I should be there, that my destiny was to meet once more with him, even if he did not remember me because he hated me so much that he had erased me from his mind.

I decided to believe that this was a new opportunity for us, to start from scratch and try to do things right this time, I took courage and went into that room. I did not pay attention to the name assigned to me, for the moment I was very busy thinking about how to approach him, maybe in his subconscious was still a flash of what I had meant in his life, if it existed, it was because his love for me was too strong to forget me at all.

I saw him sitting at the bar, I could see his back right away, despite having more people around him, I knew him perfectly. In my mind I searched for something ingenious to get him talking, for the first time my ingenuity failed me, so when I was at his height, I released the first thing my mouth wanted.

-Are you free to tell me your anecdote of hatred for Christmas?

His gaze hardened for a second to immediately soften, I knew him so well that I knew his temper and sometimes interruptions bothered him. He smiled at me and I knew right away that he really liked what he was seeing, that smile was the real one and not the one that he dedicated every day at work.

-Anecdote? There's nothing to tell, prude queen.

We both laughed at the name assigned to me, he because he found it funny and I because it was the opposite of me. If I were the prude queen, I would never have lost the love of my life.

-And you are?

I asked him more to take conversation than to know the name assigned to him, I knew perfectly who he was.

– Elvis Bowie.

The laughter that we both released was hysterical, always laughing at the small things, always living and enjoying every second. I remembered the shirt he had given me from David Bowie and my heart was squeezed, so I immediately blocked that memory so as not to let in the sadness.

-Well Elvis, notice that until a couple of years ago this was the most awaited date for me, but last year my father gave me the terrible news that he was going to divorce my mother, which made my life completely turn around and become a date that I never want to arrive. What about you? To what do we owe your income to this select club?

I improvised with the story of my parents, they really had divorced, but I learned to live with it, obviously I could not tell him that I hated Christmas because it made me miss him more than ever.

-Something similar, it has to do with my parents. They did not divorce, they just left me, they disappeared a rainy night in a plane accident and from that date it will never be the same again this day.

I could not prevent my eyes from filling with tears; I remember perfectly when I found out what happened. He did not remember that I had been by his side that I never left him alone; it killed me that he did not know that I had never left him alone.

We changed the subject and I felt the time fly by, as always when we were together, laughter, sarcasm and anecdotes could not miss. It was like being together in our relationship, only he did not remember that he ever loved me.

The candlelight dinner was epic; it was not our first dinner as well. Once I prepared a surprise for him in an old hotel in the city of Guadalajara, I surprised him with a dinner prepared by me and the whole room full of candles, like a romantic one that wanted to surprise the love of her life. When it was 12 and it was Christmas officially, we did not know what to do and I saw his indecision, so I decided to break that uncomfortable moment.

-Happy day we met. - I said, but I thought happy day that we met again.

-It's true, today we fulfill one day of that.

Something that I loved about that party was that the DJ pleased the requests of each one of those present, so I decided to run to ask for one of the most emblematic songs of our relationship. I felt cheating because I remembered everything about him and he did not remember me at all, but what else was cheating. In war and in love everything is valid and since I was there, I could not fight for him.

- What song did you ask? - He asked with great curiosity, always so meticulous I thought.

-You'll see it right now that you'll dance with me. - I said and saw his face of surprise.

-Dance? I do not dance even with two extra feet.

-Will you reject an abandoned woman on Christmas Eve?

I took his hand and made a bow as when a man invited a woman to dance as soon as I heard that the song, I asked him. I took his neck, to feel him closer to me and he immediately surrounded my waist with his arms, as in the old days, he did not like to dance, but he always did it for me. He had sung me with that horrible voice that song, at that moment I cried so much and today I wanted to do it again before that memory, but I had to control myself or he would think I was crazy. When I put that song I wanted to try to make his heart remember me, his eyes saw me as they did when we were together, so I decided to approach him to tempt him to kiss me, I watched his look and then I did not see his heart remind me, he was just a happy man to have met a beautiful woman at that party. The disappointment invaded me so when he was about to kiss me, I walked away slowly. That kiss would do more harm to me than to him, because it would be the confirmation that he no longer felt love for me.

-You have a girlfriend

I said, and it was not a question, it was an affirmation. I knew he had a girlfriend and he did not answer me, he could not deny it or accept it.

-Dance another one? - He asked me, and I nodded in surprise. Maybe it would be the last time we danced together.

-I would love it, but now you choose.

-It will be much better than that commercial ballad chosen by you prude queen.

-Are you sure? What do you want to bet?

I saw that some of those crazy ideas that came to mind happened to him, but he did not feel comfortable enough to tell me about them.

While he was returning from making his request to the DJ, I wrote on a napkin the song I guessed he had asked for, sometimes he was very predictable. He approached me and I extended that napkin.

-You can leave it on the table.

He took it in a hurry and wrapped his beer with it, we went back to the dance floor and although everyone danced raucously, we for some reason were still stuck to each other.

-Do you know that song?

-No, but it sounds very tender. -I immediately answered him, although with a lie. Obviously, I knew that song.

When the music ended, he brushed his lips with mine for a second and immediately felt happiness, but followed by an immense pain, so I did not want to be with him again, it was not fair to deceive him so much. I walked away and took his arm to take him back to the table; I took my glass of wine to cushion the pain I felt at that moment.

-Look.

I took the napkin from his beer and showed it to him. I saw his shudder when he read that simple word, but at the same time so significant for both because it was that song, our song.

"Tenderness"

-It cannot be, how did you know? Did the DJ tell you?

I smiled and put my fingers over his mouth to be quiet, I knew it was time to leave, maybe together, I wanted that deep inside me, I did not care about the pain that could cause me.

-Let's dance one last before we leave. -I asked.

-Of course. He answered without hesitation; I saw his emotion in his eyes. -Which one we chose? - he asked immediately.

-I choose it, you'll like it, I'm sure. What's more, it will make you cry.

-Impossible, and less now that I'm so happy with you here, if it makes me cry, I promise to play it on the day of our wedding. - He answered without thinking and I smiled because, although he did not know, that was the song that we always wanted to dance at our wedding.

-Wedding? We are already getting married and we barely met, but well you said, that will be the waltz of your wedding if you cry.

I took him by the hand and led him to the dance floor to dance Major Tom, that song that shook us so much, once again our bodies stuck together, I felt my body shudder at every note of that song as I closed my eyes and imagined that wedding we never had. When I opened them I saw that he cried, he also felt like me, with my hands I cleaned those sacred tears for me, at least that weeping was not of pain because of my fault, but that his heart had reminded me with that song and had felt me once more.

-So, you don't cry steel man? - I said to lighten that intense moment.

He invited me to see the sunrise at his side, I knew that he loved that moment because I had once lived it with him, in a past Christmas. Without hesitation I thought maybe he could remind me, if I helped him, remember with his heart. Just when we were picking up our things, his cell phone rang, and I noticed his nervousness when he saw who was calling. He wanted to pretend he was going to the bathroom and away from me he answered the call. Instantly I knew that it must be his girlfriend, he was too transparent. The bubble I was in broke up and reality invaded me. He hated me so much to erase me forever from his mind, me and everything lived together, and I could not expose myself to feel that pain. There is nothing worse than to be forgotten.

- Is the chariot about to become a pumpkin? - I said trying to joke when he returned from his call. I was not going to pretend I was stupid; I had never done it before, and I was not going to start at that moment.

- It was my girlfriend who just arrived in the city, drove at night and left her family to come see me.

- The staff is very high, impossible to overcome, how lucky you are dude.

I said that with a broken heart, because I had done more things for him than that gesture that she had just had. I approached and gave him a kiss, with all the feeling of a final goodbye, I owed me, and I owed it to the man who had once loved me so much. It was not easy to get away from his lips, but the decision was made, it was the goodbye I had asked so much for our relationship. He wanted to say something, but I did not let him, and I put my fingers on his lips and then run out of that place. The further I got away from him, the more I felt the misery in which I had been plunged since we separated. He did not notice that I was protected from the rain in the garage of the house next to the room where the party was, in case he went out to look for me he would not find me and continue with his life, his look searched me everywhere while I tried to contain myself so as not to run weak to his arms. My life did not make sense if he was not with me.

December 25, 2017.

Many people, when Christmas approaches, get excited automatically, I start to feel dread, I do not know why, but to see the Christmas trees and Christmas music and all the ritual that comes from the shops full of spheres of all colors and materials, reindeers of glass or wood, candles, bottles of cider, exchanges of gifts, everything seems aberrant.

My father loved Christmas, was the time of the year when we could spend more time together.

I do not understand, how I hate something that I loved so much, and it was not only because of the Christmas Eve gifts, but because of that dinner in which it was an obligation to be all together and share those moments that only occur in a home, sometimes extended with the presence of close relatives such as uncles or cousins or sometimes only the four members of this family, small in size but big in love.

But I do not know what happened, the cold chills me overnight, the trees in the streets irritate me, the alcohol makes me depressed at this time, the whiteness of the snow disturbs me, the carols are a roar in my ears , the exchanges of gifts bore me, the Christmas cards were unpleasant to my eyes, the idea of a dinner with loved ones bores me, my leg falls too heavy to sleep, to see the shops full of Christmas articles makes me lose my sanity before the commercialization of an event that was once divine and today is nothing. The poinsettia flower makes me allergic so I started being a few meters away, the leaves of the trees irritate my eyes, the pastorals are so repetitive and monotonous, the births do not represent an artistic work for me, but something trivial and routine, the holiday parties are just a bunch of drunk people with the pretext of representing that passage of the Bible.

Anyway, I think everything related to these dates makes me allergic. I do not know, nor can I remember why I started to run away from these celebrations.

And when it seemed I had found a reason not to hate this date that once filled me with so much joy, the perfect night with a perfect woman followed by an incredible dawn was interrupted with the arrival of Alejandra. It would have been very ungrateful of me and disloyal not to have answered Ale's call and continue my night with that lovely woman who had impressed me in a few hours. Perhaps this Christmas, the negative feeling towards this day will worsen as I feel a glimmer of hope in her blue gaze and in her unusual way of being that fascinated me, and having lost her, I would never know her name at least.

Alejandra slept while I brought back to my mind all that I disliked about Christmas, staring at a flame warming my coffee prepared with all my love for her that once again had not left me alone in the saddest moments of my life. That form of hundreds of colors in red and yellow, that deforms any object seeing it in a translucent form through it, diffusing itself with each wake of its flame.

Thus, the slender body of Alejandra lying on the bed was diffused through that fire, which reminded me of the flame of the Christmas fireplace in my home, waving with a flag of peace and happiness.

Feeling the warmth of that flame reminded me of my mother's warmth at dawn every Christmas, she was so similar to Alejandra in her cares, in her peaceful nature, how I missed her smile that was my best medicine since childhood, how I needed her smile when we opened the gifts, my best gift would be to see her again, which I knew was impossible, but I wanted it more than ever at this time. Her arms always comfortable filling with security at any time, giving me the courage to face every problem in life from everyday children as an exam or the unusual juveniles' hangovers after a night of partying and watch over my dream.

Sometimes it seemed to me also unintelligible why so much aberration on my part at this time, perhaps unconsciously had an image in my mind that I could not visualize understandably. I do not know, but I stopped liking Christmas and more after not knowing where the prude queen was.

April 23, 2018. Coatzacoalcos, Veracruz

- Becca?!

- Alejandra? What are you doing here?!

- You are the crazy woman who attacked my Eduardo?

The anger of Alejandra for the mistreatment to Eduardo was diminishing, happened to be completely surprised but, above all, to feel that weight on her shoulders, to know that that woman standing in front of her could at any moment snatch what she loved most. She felt quite scared, her body felt a chill starting from the tips of her fingers to her chest to imagine that Eduardo could realize who was the woman with whom he had discussed in that place and recapture the memories of her. That's why she decided not to fight and try to be as civilized as possible, after all, as long as she did not have contact with him everything was going excellent and even in the worst case, as that day of accidentally finding her, he did not even recognize her, go back to that sick relationship was impossible. So, she relaxed while the debate with Becca continued.

-Yes, I'm sorry, I saw him from afar since he came in, here we used to eat together almost every day, it was our place of reference, the most symbolic point of our relationship that, I went crazy to hear him complain, but, above all, I lost the control to see that he had not the slightest idea who I was, after having spent the best hours of our lives together and now being a complete stranger. Is that fair? - Becca replied, beckoning her to sit down at a table with her to chat while asking for coffee for both. - You have no idea how hard it is to live away from him, sometimes I thought about killing myself, please Alejandra give him back to me, I'll do whatever you want, but give him back to me, you know he's always been mine, I'm the love of his life.

-You, now he does not even know who you are, and everything were thanks to you. How do you want me to return him to you if it is not merchandise, it is the love of my life and I have always wanted and him, you decided to change him for another man?

-Please I beg.

The waiters looked at each other and the occasional diner had no idea what the two women sitting at the far table were discussing, while they were arguing heatedly.

Becca's face flushed and wrinkled by the great courage she felt, was transformed in moments, that frown was moving down, falling to an unprecedented level in her life, disconnected, with a sadness that could breathe around the place, the diners could notice it and even more when a tear slowly trickled down her cheek.

The irrational anger that caused her to see that Eduardo did not even recognize her, went to a state of stillness, defeated by seeing that engagement ring on the ring finger of Alejandra, killed her in life.

-When is the wedding?

Alejandra noticed the reason of her change when observing the lost look of Becca in her left hand and for more that she tried to change the subject making herself the fool, stumbled and had to answer her.

-We still do not know, he just asked me to marry him at Christmas.

Becca no longer had a way to contain the gale of tears in her eyes and got up from the table and walked hurriedly to the other exit of the room where Eduardo did not see her, or she to him. Her heart was broken, that Christmas they had spent together at that party where both used pseudonyms and although he did not recognize her, she knew that his love was not dead. Just after it, he proposed to Alejandra, everything in Becca's life was over. Alejandra tried to stop her even screaming at her from afar asking for forgiveness. But Becca left.

May 27, 2018

That day the pain had become unbearable, in the morning paper I found the note where they congratulated Eduardo and Alejandra for their upcoming wedding on November 1st of this same year, my heart could not stand anymore, and I felt totally destroyed. I walked through the streets of Coatzacoalcos and every corner brought me memories of him, every corner caused me a pain never felt before. How can you survive the loss of the love of your life? Especially when you know that you are responsible.

From the day I lost him to this day, I also thought a million times to go to the doctor and erase him from my mind, my heart and my miserable existence, but I could not, because to erase him would be like erasing me, I could not erase the most beautiful thing I've ever lived, to erase him would be like taking from my life the only good thing I've ever had. No, I would not erase him, I will take each of the moments by his side to the grave.

I walked feeling his absence with each step I took, wanting to feel his hand taking mine and leading the way back home, there was only a void between my fingers.

That afternoon was rainy, as we liked it. People watched me as they passed by with their big umbrellas as if I were crazy. Crazy for getting wet? I thought they were stupid, water does not burn, but neither does it take away feelings. Simply the gray sky and the excessive rain combined perfectly with my feelings, I had always wanted to die on such a day. It seems macabre, but it was the perfect day to cease to exist.

I stopped in front of the cafeteria where we always bought our chai tea, looked inside and my eyes did not find him. A part of me wanted to see him and so maybe I would convince myself not to do what I was planning, but it was no sign of him. So many memories came to my mind that I closed my eyes so I could feel them more powerful. Chai tea was something of ours, something to be able to enjoy in a day of calm or a day of those that even breathing took time away. On each trip we asked for it and we compared it with that of this cafeteria, it was like a ritual that brought us closer to home. My heart broke even more as I remembered each trip, each night sleeping together, the warmth of his back against my cheek as I hugged him, and he took my hand. Sleeping with him had been sacred; waking up at his side was being at home no matter the place or city where we were. He was my home and since I had lost him, I felt that I no longer belonged to anything, much less anyone. I felt helpless.

I walked for hours, reliving every moment by his side, there were so many... even the fights now seemed silly. Maybe at some point I felt abandoned or ignored, but that was not justification for what I did and that led me to lose him forever. He was always there, although sometimes he went away, now I know he was always there. Now that he is not there, I realize that by losing him, I lost my life. I never considered myself weak, but today I was completely destroyed, worse than a war zone in the instant after being destroyed by a bomb.

If I could not get him back, what was the point of continuing with this pain? I wanted to finish it. That thought made me walk faster, I wanted to get home and be free of so much pain, free to be able to fly. Maybe the sky was a place where the longing that I felt at this moment would no longer exist.

Even though it was a cool day, I did not feel it. My body began to stop perceiving reality due to the great depression in which I was. After several hours walking around the city and remembering each moment with him, in a happier, more beautiful and brighter life, I arrived home. The sun was beginning to get in and I hurried to turn on the lights, I had always feared the darkness, although my life had already lost its light.

I sat in the living room and wanted to cry, but my eyes had no more tears to expel. The pain in my chest was more intense than ever and even then, I was already dry. Maybe it was the sensation that imminent death causes you or in my subconscious I knew that I should not cry anymore, that everything was about to end. I did not want to change my clothes to something dry, an illness I did not care anymore, so soaked I went to my room and took out that little box of

Dilatrend medicine, the one that the cardiologist had prescribed for me so many years ago and that now had become a weapon , instead of relief.

I looked through my window and it was still raining, I smiled instantly thinking that it was the perfect day to die.

I always believed that people who commit suicide are weak, cowardly, that there was no reason in the world to take their own lives. Today I knew that there was, it was him. Knowing that he did not love me anymore, that he would spend the rest of his life with another woman, that with her he would have the children that he and I always planned to have, that he had decided to erase me, to throw me out of his life as if I had been a garbage to forget and never to remember its existence, immediately my body was filled with courage. Maybe I was a coward when I took my life, but he had been a coward when he wiped me out completely. He was the first to kill me, now it was my turn to give the final thrust, there is no point in living when my only reason for doing so no longer wants me in his life. Without him, nothing makes sense. Without him, I cannot continue living. That is the way I love him, he is my everything, from the first hour of the day, until the last hour of the night.

I opened my closet and took out a bottle of mezcal, we loved drinking mezcal together. Apart from beer, mezcal was our favorite drink to enjoy together. I wanted to say goodbye to him honoring our memories.

I took Dilatrend's box, 14 pills that in an overdose cause your pulsations to drop unconscious and take you to those warm arms of death, where I will no longer have to endure his absence, where this love no longer will consume me day and night, where I will be able to love him eternally, without pain.

I dressed in the blue shirt he gave me to keep during the first football game we saw together, it did not smell like him anymore, but it was as close as I could get to his essence. I uncapped the bottle and took the first drink, immediately felt the heat go through my throat and fill my body with warmth for a few seconds. From my bag I took out that farewell letter I wrote to him, maybe one day he would read it and he could forgive me. I placed it on the desk and saw his name written, I knew that the moment had arrived. I could not be with him and I could not live without him, it was too painful.

I put all the pills inside my fist, I closed my eyes and I started that farewell ritual of my love, of my life and I welcomed that friend called death.

First pill, I remembered that time when we were 16 years old and we lost virginity together. There I knew that I wanted to spend the rest of my life with him.

His smile appeared in my mind with the second pill, that arrogant and adorable smile that I loved since the first time I saw it.

His smell flooded my senses once again after the third, that smell of perfume and if you stopped to breathe close to his skin, you could feel his natural aroma, the one that reminded me that I was at home.

He was in front of me while I took the pills one by one, little by little I felt my pulse go down. His image, his memory, his presence flooded my mind. Suddenly I felt that I was not walking alone anymore, he took my hand and guided me in the end, and I felt at peace. Once again, I saw his smile and I was back home...

-I love you.

May 29, 2018, Coatzacoalcos, Veracruz.

I have always felt a great sadness when attending a funeral, so I try to avoid going to the maximum, and it has nothing to do with the death of my parents years ago or with their heartbreaking funeral after the accident, this goes back years back, maybe since childhood, I could not know, but the death of someone always causes me much pain. It could be a consequence of the person I loved most when I was six years old, my grandmother, who left me a bitter experience, but I do not believe it because since I was a teenager when I was accompanying my parents, even though I did not know the deceased, I ended up with a sea of crying. It made me so sad, that one day I remember going to the burial of a man who worked in the construction company with my father and that I had no opportunity to cross a word with him in life.

His death was not even tragic, I think he was already a couple of years with a chronic condition that I do not remember what it was.

It is that moment when everyone says goodbye to take the coffin to the funeral, in which my heart cracks, to see all the family members with tears and cries of pain, it infects me and makes me cry too.

I remember the girl sitting next to me in the black chairs in the mortuary; she approached me and told me with a sarcastic tone that why I was crying if that person was not even a relative or an acquaintance of mine.

I found her comment so stupid that I answered the first thing that came to mind.

-The human beings are so unconscious that we cry when seeing in a movie when someone dies and when we are in a real situation, where a human being has just passed away, we wonder illogically what you just questioned me. How is it possible that we think that it is valid to cry in a movie with a fictional death and in a real one, not?

She was silent and went to sit at the other end.

Alejandra knew of my aberration to the funeral processions and even so she asked me to accompany her, must be someone very precious to her because the news had caused her great nostalgia. She had not eaten anything all day and had suspended all her activities in the office as a designer.

That's why I could not refuse to accompany her, indeed, I did not even sketch any disagreement, I just said yes, that she would let me know what time she was picking me up.

It was Friday and I did not have much work, so I decided to stay home while I waited a few hours for Alejandra.

I checked the newspaper and noticed that there were more obituaries than usual, that name sounded familiar to me, so

I decided to call Alejandra to ask her friend's name to make sure she was the one with the many obituaries.

- How did you tell me your friend was called?

-Rebeca Hess Cavanhi, why the question?

-There are several obituaries of her in the newspaper; it must be from a well-known family. How did she die?

-She committed suicide. - I felt her voice change and she cut herself a little, watching her cry, so I did not want to torment her anymore, she must have been a great friend of hers, so I said goodbye to her.

Even that news made me shudder, why a young woman, so beautiful, as I could see in some photos of her obituaries, had been able to make that irremediable decision.

It happened to me when I attended some funeral and some tears escaped from my cheeks, for someone I did not have the pleasure of knowing, while I drank some coffee and finished checking the newspaper.

I was struck by that date in the upper corner of each page, a day like today, May 29, twenty-four years ago my grandmother had died, my adoration. But that was not the most shocking of the date, but also a day like today, but 30 years ago, my grandfather had died. In fact, at some point in my life I thought that I too would die on that same date, which was the family's destiny.

I did not have a single black shirt in my closet, in fact, I do not think I have had one in recent years; I have never liked black and white. For a funeral it is customary to wear black or white, but I did not have either, the only white shirts I had were those I wore with a suit and tie. The only thing that occurred to me was to wear one of those shirts and I remembered at that moment that thick black tie of fine Chinese silk, bought for some occasion I did not remember. So, I could use the black suit used in formal events and so wear the color that warranted the occasion.

I unhooked all the clothes from the closet and opened the drawer where I kept that dark tie. I polished my shoes with a special brush I had in the closet and I was ready waiting for Alejandra to come and pick me up.

I put some music, I still did not understand how all the songs in my playlist could be erased, if I was supposed to keep them in the cloud, I did not like anything.

Blessed technology, I decided to look for the selected lists of friends I knew, but nothing pleased me, that crazy idea crossed my mind, although it did not have to be, so I saw it more as a posthumous tribute. I decided to look in that music application for the selection of songs from Alejandra's deceased friend. I typed her name to check if she had any selection in the application and I was glad to see that she did, so I gave it play and started listening to some of her favorite songs. All were commercial and recent, as I called them teenagers.

She had a folder that was titled "For You", apparently there was someone who moved the mat as my aunts said when a person managed to please you too sentimentally.

I sat on the terrace of my apartment and I served myself a little more Colombian coffee that I still had from my trip to Bogotá. I touched the selection of that dear friend of Ale and raised the volume to a level before the maximum.

The first song started and as a flow came out of my face an infinity of tears before the sadness that caused me, Prince singing "Purple Rain", that old song had already many years that I did not listen and did not know why it was a fascinating ballad .

"I never want to cause you any pain. I only wanted to see you laughing in the Purple Rain."

I gained nostalgia, my mind always listening to that song; imagine dancing very slowly in the rain to a lovely woman hugging me.

But, above all, that ending was heartbreaking, all the fibers of my body moved those sharp sounds without meaning, but evoked pain, probably losing someone, who loves as never before.

In that I was in a trance with that song and crying when a few seconds before the end the doorbell rang. It was Alejandra who had already arrived to pick me up to go to the funeral.

We arrived a little before sunset to that beautiful house located on the seashore, fortunately because the last rays of the sun allowed us to admire that garden full of bougainvillea coloring the path until we reach the main entrance. How beautiful was the bright sunset in the background with those two hills bathing the sea with their shadow and all around the house flowered in lilac? Although there were hundreds of meters of distance between the house and the landscape, the visual effect made all those fused images look like a single image, rays of the sun, waves of the sea, reflection in the water, green hills, lilac bougainvillea, impeccable architecture from the mansion, the breeze added one more effect to another of the senses, not just the view. I liked that house very much from the first moment that I observed it in the distance when we were a few meters from the entrance. I felt trapped by its nature every meter that we entered, I felt very calm, something difficult to explain, but I felt too comfortable to enter there. I remembered my house, it had some similar architectural details like that elegant red, green and white marble that my parents and I liked so much, it reminded us of the one that covered the capital of Florence that we admired together when I was only 13 years old. I thought I would be one of the most elegant in the place, but it was not like that, most of that aristocratic family wore impeccable dark suits of the most famous and expensive brands in the world. But who would like to release these outfits in such a sad ovation? I did it because I had no other choice; it was my only black outfit.

The deceased's parents were tearing their heart with delirious cries of suffering to see her again.

I did not even think about approaching them to give them my condolences, I would not have the courage to endure that.

Her father, of notorious German features, very white skin and blue eyes the color of the sea, and his mother with a blonde hair, walked slowly to where I was, surely they went to the toilets that were located behind where I was leaning against the wall while I waited for Alejandra to offer her condolences to the older brother of her great friend Becca.

I crossed the isle to serve me a loaded coffee, because I did not know how long we would be at the wake. I took a drink and every drop that flowed inside of me restored my life and increased the sleep that could appear.

-Thank you for coming, Eduardo

I burned myself and listen to those words that seemed to be addressed to me. It was Rebecca's dad reaching out to greet me and hug me, I had no choice but to hug him the same and feel his chest heaving with crying and I gave my condolences, as well as her mother clinging to me sobbing some words that barely could distinguish with the voice cut from so much crying.

-She adored you.

I thought I heard those words, but I thought I misunderstood.

-Do not know how sorry I am, my deepest sympathy.

-We know, Eduardo, we know.

How did they know my name? And they left there in the direction of their daughter's coffin.

If I felt uncomfortable in that place where I did not know anyone, now I felt worse, even pain had given me, not physical pain, but that pain that is felt in the soul with the loss of a loved one.

I went to Alejandra to ask her when we would retire.

-I do not know Eduardo, if you like I can take you to your house, I will stay here until dawn, I cannot miss these last moments with Becca.

-Why do you think I'm going to leave you here alone? I'll accompany you; if I feel sleepy, I'll go to rest for a while in the car.

But it did not get tired; on the contrary, one more cup of coffee was enough to not close my eyes all night.

I began to review the photo albums that Becca's parents had in their house and made available to the attendees in the room where the funeral was taking place.

Being there I felt a great emotion, a pleasant sensation.

How beautiful Becca was, how could I never know her if she was such a friend of Alejandra.

I settled into a chair in the living room, drinking a little more coffee and delicious bread, offered for the companions at the wake.

That voice with a strong German accent surprised me again.

-Eduardo, I do not believe much in the theories of life after death, but I think it would please you to say goodbye to her.

I had no words to express what I felt, but, above all, to approach that coffin and express feelings to a stranger. But, if she was a friend of Alejandra, the woman who would be my wife for the rest of my life, she was also a friend of mine, even if I did not have the pleasure of having met her.

-Yes, I'll do it, I'm just waiting for Alejandra to approach her.

And that big man hugged me again.

-Thank you, son, you do not know how I thank you for coming.

It was just a pretext to wait for Alejandra, since she had already done so since we arrived at the place, but I could not think of any other excuse to seize courage and not do so at that moment.

That old man walked away, and his face improved when I told him that I would go to say goodbye to his daughter.

I felt extremely nervous about doing this ritual that I did not do with my relatives when I had gone to their funeral, but I had the commitment to do it, that broken voice of a man hurt by the departure of his daughter motivated me to fulfill that sacred promise.

I got up straight to the coffin, which I had not approached since we arrived at the house. I adjusted my tie on the road, I had to look impeccable, I climbed a step of the pedestal where she was.

They had chosen the best photo for this moment, I had the opportunity to meet her at that moment, her smile was incredible, and she must have been an incredible woman.

What a bitter moment, maybe the biggest I've ever had in my life, I began to sweat nervously and could not contain the rivers that threatened to come out violently from my eyes, it was impossible to do so, in a moment I was a sea of tears.

As much as I tried not to draw attention to not worry Alejandra I did not achieve it, all the assistants looked at me, some worried, others nervous, others with morbid, others with compassion, others with skepticism, but in the end my so heartbreaking and irrepressible crying it did not go unnoticed.

That smile in each corner of her lips was perfect, radiated joy and those golden curls dull any beautiful ray of light, sad to see no more those gestures and more when someone had been able to observe them in life.

Sad to hear no more that soft, tenuous voice, moving like a perfect compass of an emotional and rhythmic melody. Sad to not have drunk with her the last glass of wine that December 25. Sad to have fallen in love in a few hours of her for feeling that I knew her for life and every word fit in me as perfectly accurate darts in her goal. Sorry not to know her name until today.

If only I had seen that dawn with her. At least it would not die that eternal memory without a name and a surname, at least I could settle her name and bring her flowers from time to time, of the many that I could send her in life, and remove that vulgar, but funny nickname with which I met her, prude queen.

May 30, 2018, 05:57 a.m.

There came a time when pain overcame me, I had never felt that in my life.

Alejandra noticed and immediately ran to get me up after falling to my knees in front of that coffin. As always, she did not ask me anything, she just hugged me and consoled me, she knew something very painful was happening to me, but at that moment for her the main thing was my state of mind.

She took me to that chair near the front door of the house and there she gave me a drink of water and checked my vital signs, she was very worried, a few minutes passed, and I could control myself.

Almost half an hour passed so that I could breathe again normal and my voice could articulate some words, it was then the ideal time to talk to Alejandra and tell her about that Christmas Eve when I had the opportunity to meet her great friend, Becca.

She smiled and showed me her understanding for the pain I felt at having met her friend who had passed away and whose name I did not know, until Alejandra told me so. Moreover, I even noticed a great relief in telling that story, as if she had imagined some other difficult story that I had revived with Becca, even in the story I confessed how much I had liked to meet her and it had seemed like an incredibly beautiful and nice woman.

-I understand, Becca was irresistible, the perfect woman.

-I imagine she was very nice and very beautiful; I spent a great evening with her, what a pity that she made this decision.

-And, even so, I only met a man who she was really in love with all her soul, but she left him because of existential problems that she had.

-He must have been a very lucky guy.

-He is, later I tell you the full story of that strange romance, I have to go with Becca's parents because they are calling me to go talk with them. - In the distance, those elders called her.

-Yes, do not worry, go, I'll wait for you here, I'm better.

While she was talking to the mourners, at the door I was surprised to see Nacho enter Becca's house.

-What are you doing here? Did you know the deceased?

He got a little nervous, loaded his usual instrument, his keyboard and the jacket he played with in his band.

-Yes, Eduardo, I came with the band to play some songs for the funeral.

-Songs? But you play rock.

-Yes, I know, but we will play some classic instrumental ballads and, finally, when they say goodbye to her, her family will carry out Becca's last request, which she left in a posthumous letter where she asked us to play her favorite song when she was buried. But as there will be no burial, but cremation, then we will do it at the moment they say goodbye to her to take her to the crematory after the mass.

-So, will not there be a burial?

-No, her ashes will stay here at her house, in her room, that's what her parents decided to feel close to her.

-It must be a very sad moment for everyone in the family.

- Yes, even, Jaime, Becca's brother is going to play the bass with us, although he must be devastated to lose his sister.

-The bass player, is he Becca's brother? He must feel terrible to play.

-On the contrary, that will make him feel better and allow him to fulfill Becca's last will, which was his adoration; she always cared for him and convinced his parents to let him study music instead of being an engineer like his father.

All of the group were arriving little by little until completing the band of seven members, they began to play classical music that Becca's parents liked, with a nice sound of the electric guitar and the bass, one that another note provoked in the sir to return to that heartbreaking cry to later calm down, perhaps not so much for the comfort of those present, but because of the lack of physical strength to continue with that attrition.

It was already 6 am in the morning, the first rays of the sun reflected on the gleaming golden coffin where Becca was and touched her golden hair; she still looked radiant and alive.

At 8 a.m. was a mass of present body and from there, finishing the last goodbye to take her to the crematorium, our assistance ended, which made me feel a bit of relief, I could not bear to see how they cremated Becca after having enthralled with her smile and abandon me that way. The good thing was that the ritual ended there.

At times I felt again what it feels like when a loved one is lost, and the best memories come to mind, and I sobbed again. Although all my memories of Becca were one night, a magical and unforgettable one, where I was captivated by each of her details. She was the perfect woman, how could she do that, and when I dressed me up with this thought I would cry again and again without stopping, until fatigue weakened my body and face.

The mass was another ordeal, but there were only a few minutes left for the farewell, and I would go to my house to rest from this unforeseen nightmare that I was living and that I did not want to continue suffering. However, I thanked God for this unfortunate coincidence, if I had never heard from her again. At least I could say goodbye by her name and stare at her face.

The priest gave the last words of consolation to the mourners who were already calmer with that cult and everyone was preparing to go to the coffin to say goodbye and then take her to the crematorium.

Saying goodbye to her was a stab in the depths of my soul, I will never forget when I approached and I saw her there, still dead she wore that incomparable smile, at times I wanted her to wake up and see everything was a mistake, refusing to accept not seeing her again, but I had to resign myself and I did so, I left a white rose on the glass that covered her master smile, and I retired.

They all finished saying goodbye and the group went from playing that quiet music to singing that rock melody that seemed familiar to me.

-This song is dedicated to my little sister, my beloved Becca. - It was heard in the microphone to express Jaime.

The moment they took the coffin, his father approached me.

-Becca asked us to deliver this to you in the letter she left us.

He handed me a book with a cover in the shape of a poinsettia flower, with a lilac background, whose title was "Always you", the author did not sound familiar to me, Juan Manuel Rodríguez Caamaño. I immediately opened the first page of that novel, at the same instant that her parents said goodbye to me and left for the crematorium.

It had a very nice dedication for me. That detail had me dripping down my nostrils and smiling at the same time, for all the incredibly beautiful moments we could have lived if we had had more time. For a moment, I condemned her for not giving me that opportunity, but in a flash, I forgave her because she was too adorable to have any bad memories of her. It was so fantastic that she could have known exactly who I was, and I did not have that privilege of knowing her in life.

"To Eduardo:

I dedicate this novel to you; it is my favorite for several reasons. First, because I read it when I discovered that your gaze looked at me with the same affection with which I looked at you too. And every detail of this novel I imagined with you ".

Those words had me screaming in tears as I had never done in my life, especially because that night had also been unforgettable for her, so she confessed in the dedication of that book.

At one end of the room, Becca's brother cried as he played the interpretation of each chord of that song.

"I don't know where we are going now"

"The second reason, because I think if one day, one of the two would get ahead we would find ourselves in another life as in this beautiful novel, I do not know why I am so sure of it, but I imagine that attraction so strong that we have, it gives me that hope and it can be a good omen ".

Those chords were no longer unknown to me and that letter seemed like an order from her to me.

"Take a look at me now"

"Take a look at me noooooowwwww"

In that place of the party, it was where I heard her for the first time, that's why she felt that I should turn her over to see when we met, as if it were an order from her mind to mine, look at me now.

"Take a look at me now"

And I looked at the coffin for the last time and more tears came, I do not know where they come from, I was already empty of so much crying.

"I love you, Eduardo, happy anniversary; I hope it's the first of all eternity because I want to be with you all my life."

I heard her voice like an echo in my mind, saying those words over and over again, vibrating louder and louder, shaking me as if they hit me physically in the head.

Lifetime
Lifetime

"The treatment works perfectly if you avoid having contact with the other party, not because you can remember something when you see her, in fact, you will not even recognize her having her face less than an inch, however, she may have some very strong memory of you or even some memory of yours that you have returned, that is even stronger, against that we do not have any medicine, because it is programmed by you not by her and when she returns it, you gave her a very strong weapon so that you can never forget her."

So, you can never forget her.

So, you can never forget her.

And to those details we cannot have access unless you ask for all those memories or you steal them from where she kept them. Which is very complex, it's easier to just walk away.

Anniversary? If we only met one night.

Take a look at me now

That chorus drilled into my ears, repeating itself over and over again while the song was dying.

"April 8, 2012"

At that moment, seeing the date of that dedication, images began to appear in my head without meaning, images of me in places I did not remember, and she was always there. Inside the book there was a letter.

Hello my love:

I am writing this letter because it is the last time you will know about me, the last memory that you may decide to erase. Life without you has been a hell, love you and cannot touch you, see you and cannot tell you who I am, cannot fight for you and your forgiveness has robbed me the little life I had left since we are not together.

I always believed in heaven and I implore God that there is where he takes me after taking this decision of not existing without you. From my heaven I will love you and take care of you until it is time for us to rediscover the beautiful eternity and maybe, by the time it passes, you have forgiven me, I also hope that in the last seconds of your life you will remember me, just as I am sure, you will be my last thought as I breathe my last breath.

I would like to go back and change all my mistakes; I would like to have a life by your side full of children, grandchildren and many years of love. In this life we will not be able to, but I am sure that in the next one we will meet again, and we will try again. I will wait anxiously for that new story that we have to live together. Remember that you are the love of my life, only you and always you.

Physically I have already left, but I will always be by your side and I know that you can feel me at every moment if you just close your eyes and let your heart guide you. From my heaven I will also watch over you because that love that you gave me could never be equaled to another you give, because in another woman you will look for my skin, my eyes and my stupid smile that you loved so much. Because

I know that even though you erased me from your mind, your heart reminds me.

Do not feel guilty, this was my decision. A decision I made for not being able to live without you, because without you my existence stopped making sense. My betrayals led me to lose you and this is the final consequence.

I'll be waiting for you love of my life, while we meet again, be happy that I'll take care of you from up there.

I will always be part of you.

I love you forever…

Your Becca

At that moment I felt that I was suffocating, I was short of breath, at that moment I could die, physically and emotionally I felt shattered, every muscle in my body collapsed with so much pain,

Why?

Noooooooooo,

Damn

A thousand times damn

I fell in love again

I ran to the garden of the house so no one would see me cry, but it was no longer a heartrending crying of love, it was a cry of anger, of hatred, I buried my hands in the earth and tore the grass with my nails, I wanted to tear out all the earth of the world.

I had so much courage, I had fallen in love with her again and she abandoned me, how could she do it? In that moment I went from worshiping her to detesting her, she left me for another, she cheated me with a stranger, I fell in love with her and she flees from this cowardly way.

Nooooooo! I do not forgive you; Becca I will never do it.

Not caring anymore, I started screaming like crazy in the garden.

Damn, I hate you, Alejandra ran to hug me and seeing that book in my hands she realized instantly what was happening and as always, she comforted me. But this had no remedy, she had mocked me once again, I loved her as anyone in the world. I loved her every moment of my life.

Hopefully we reincarnate as she wished, in another life, to detest her and make her suffer what I was suffering at that moment.

To tear a lip wildly for having torn me apart, those lips that were my weakness. I would give anything to have them back with mine.

Damn her!

I could have fallen in love with her hundreds of times, if I erased her on the same number of occasions, because she was the perfect woman for me, but she was gone.

EPILOGUE

Many painful events occurred in Becca's life; the divorce of her parents, the sexual abuse suffered, the loss and disappointment of the love of her life with whom she always dreamed to spend her whole life, the supposed betrayal of her friend Alejandra; that created a great void in her life.

Each head is a world, the response to multiple situations varies in each person, but although the pain can be immense, suicide is not even a solution to problems.

Becca ended her life but destroyed the lives of her parents who adored her, her brothers with whom she shared her life, Eduardo whose pain he will never forget, Alejandra who in spite of everything had a great appreciation for her, and the rest of the five continents.

Fighting against all odds would have been the most romantic option, and at least she would have had some chance of recovering Eduardo. In the long run she would have been able to make him fall in love again with her despite not having any memory in his mind about her, because for Eduardo she was the ideal woman. Sadly, she decided the option she considered most simple, even knowing that the best thing in life is what is fought for.

Taking your own life will never be an option for love, love is life.